✡ *Bra* **WESTERN**

P9-CRW-527

Large Print Bra

Brand, Max, 1892-1944.

The black signal

Stain on back. LN 3-30-01

MAY 7 1990
LPN

H N
IS B
Z H
A N
H N
A M
N. V.
G

DUE IN ~~14 DAYS~~

14 DAY LOAN

NEWARK PUBLIC LIBRARY
NEWARK, OHIO

THE
BLACK
SIGNAL

Also available in Large Print
by Max Brand:

The Gentle Desperado
Mountain Guns
The Rangeland Avenger
Trouble in Timberline
Three on the Trail
Rogue Mustang
The Trail to San Triste
Rawhide Justice
Max Brand's Stories, Volume II

THE BLACK SIGNAL

BY
MAX BRAND

G.K.HALL&CO.
Boston, Massachusetts
1987

Copyright 1925 by Street & Smith Publications, Inc.
Copyright renewed 1953 by Dorothy Faust.

All rights reserved.

Published in Large Print by arrangement with
Dodd, Mead & Company, Inc.

British Commonwealth rights courtesy of
Robert Hale Limited.

G.K. Hall Large Print Book Series.

Set in 18 pt Plantin.

Library of Congress Cataloging in Publication Data

Brand, Max, 1892–1944.
  The black signal.
  (G.K. Hall large print book series)
  1. Large type books. I. Title.
[PS3511.A87B57 1987]   813'.52   87-8674
ISBN 0-8161-4143-6 (lg. print)

ONE

I never thought that Lew Melody was to blame; but the society into which he was born was at fault. This conclusion I arrived at before the real trouble ever began, and I know that I was not alone in that feeling. Others had the same thought, though they could not express it so clearly, and when the true explosion came, to which all the rest had been minor preparations, not a voice was lifted in behalf of Lew Melody except my own—and in such matters the minister's voice is never much heeded.

No minister, in fact, is supposed to be at home in dealing with a narrative of such odd, ridiculous, and terrible events as the history of Lew Melody; but, nevertheless, I think no one is better acquainted with

1

the facts than I. At this statement Sheriff Joe Crockett would smile, I know; but to many of the details I was an eyewitness, and to all I have the testimony of fairly honest men. Some of it is my own imagining, I admit; but I have an idea that my own imaginings are perhaps truer than the facts. All our words and all our actions are only partial expressions of the thing which is in us. However, I must not forget that this is not a sermon.

But to go back to my first statement—if Lew Melody had been brought to his early manhood somewhere in the jungles of India or the wild heart of Africa—if he had had tigers and lions and leopards to contend with, he would have been a mighty hunter and a valuable member of society.

But the wilds of the West could offer to young Melody only a few grizzlies of a race which had been gun shy for half a hundred years and a scattering of pumas which were cowards by nature and by education. So Melody, with his soul of fire, turned elsewhere. He hunted among men!

But at first he was discreet. I challenge Sheriff Joe Crockett to deny that he once vowed to me that nine tenths of his hardest work was performed by the hand of young Melody! For Barneytown lay in a snug valley which pointed south toward Mexico and the Mexican trail. In the older centuries, along this trail the Comanches swept south, crossed the Rio Grande, burned, murdered, robbed, and then rode back, driving their captured herds of cattle. Along this trail, also, Mexican punitive expeditions worked north and struck with desperation, but usually in vain, at the elusive redskins. What farmer in the valley has not turned up ancient bones of cattle—and of men? And in the brown summer the old trail is marked with a dotted line of chalk—the skeletons which wolves and buzzards picked clean in the long ago.

If the railroads have turned the main channels of travel in other directions, still the old warpath of the Comanches served purposes of its own, for down it rode fugitives from American justice, and up it wandered Mexicans who had escaped across the Rio Grande. They pooled in Barneytown.

I do not mean to say that our little town was the constant resort of malefactors or that they forced us to breathe an atmosphere of crime. No, much as I differ with Sheriff Joe Crockett in many of his opinions, let me pay high tribute to him now: If he could find crime, he never lacked the courage or the strength to crush it. It was an underground river, if I may call it that, composed of a north and a south current, each of which bobbed above the surface at Barneytown for a quiet hour or two to get provisions, rest, and perhaps buy ammunition, before it slid away once more on the long trail. And it was among these that Lew Melody hunted; it was from them that he received his training.

He was a scant fourteen when the first crash came. Up to that time he had been busy in minor affairs, such as thrashing with his fists every boy in town during the winter school months when he was not at work on his uncle's ranch. But at fourteen he felt himself enough of a man to hunt for greater trouble. He went to find it in the tramp "jungle" just north of Barneytown, and he did not have to wait long for what he wanted.

Afterward, he managed to drag himself back from the hollow and onto the high road. Don Carter passed in his buckboard and brought the boy back to the town, a well-soaked mass of still running blood, from knife wounds which had searched for his vitals and missed them by a miracle. I think he was two months in bed after his adventure, but when he was questioned he refused to explain. Only when the sheriff went to him, he said through his teeth: "There was two of 'em!" But who the two were he would not say.

The reason was that he promised himself to take an ample vengeance later on. For the remainder of that year he became the most industrious, soberly quiet boy in the whole valley. Some people hoped that the lesson had been not too dearly paid for, and that Lew would be a grave man the rest of his life and one who respected the prowess as well as the rights of others. But others observed that he worked nearly all the time with knife and gun, studying ways and means of offense and defense. The very next winter he began to show the effects of these ardent studies.

Once again he repaired to the jungle, and the next day some odd stains were discovered on the clothes of young Lew Melody; while, in the jungle, there lay the body of a tall Mexican with a knife thrust in the hollow of his throat. The sheriff went straight to Lew, of course, and accused him.

5

"I dunno what you mean," said Lew, with a gracious smile. "After my lesson last year I guess I wouldn't hunt for no trouble of that kind again! Not by a long shot!"

"Look here, Lew," said Crockett, "this might have been a serious thing, I admit, if it were another man. But I have a description of this fellow from old Mexico. He was a murdering skunk down there, and they wanted him pretty bad."

"Is that so?" said Lew.

"So talk up, son," said Crockett. "There's a reward, in fact. I don't know how much!"

"I dunno what you're talking about," said Lew Melody.

And that was his attitude always. He made a point of never claiming the victories in any of these secret battles of his.

So he went on to his twenty-second year, when the fatal disaster came. I must admit that Sheriff Joe Crockett had foreseen the evil day before it arrived.

"This kid needs work for his hands," said the sheriff to me one Sunday when he had remained after church to argue with me some point in my sermon. "He's turned the crooks away. He's made this

6

valley a real bad lands for 'em. And now what'll he do?"

"He'll settle down and be a sober man!" said I, because I confess that I had always liked the boy.

"The devil he will!" said the sheriff. "Trouble is his natural element. He's got to have it. Can a fish breathe when it's out of water?"

All the prejudices of Barneytown against Melody were not entirely groundless. Perhaps you will think that, because he rid the place of the gun fighters and the Mexican knife experts, he had good grounds to expect popularity. And, as a matter of fact, he *was* popular with many, because I presume that Barneytown was as rough and as filled with hardy men as any place in the mountain desert, so that there were plenty of people—chiefly the young men— who looked upon Melody as a sort of Achilles, fated to a short but a glorious life. But there was something a little unnatural in the daring of Melody. There was something frightful in that hunger for danger which led him into perils which thrilled other men in the mere telling. How many blood feuds were started by his terrible right hand in action I cannot so

7

much as guess, but I remember a time when Barneytown grew solemn because three Mexicans, ugly-looking specimens, entered the village, declaring that they had come for the scalp of this man destroyer, this fiery Lew Melody.

I presume that a round dozen friends of that youth hunted for him to warn him of his danger; but when they found him he filled them with wonder and horror by deliberately riding out on the trail of the three—and into the night! The details of that night were never known, because Lew Melody never talked of his doings, but the three Mexicans were never seen again, and Lew came back the next morning. It was generally believed that he wounded one or more of them in the very beginning of the battle, and that after that they trusted to the fleet heels of their horses rather than to their own courage and skill. At any rate, this affair made such an immense impression upon the Mexicans—for the three were all known men—that, I think, no man south of the Rio Grande would have considered facing Melody from that moment forth. They looked upon it as suicide.

At the same time, I think the affair

ended the period during which Lew was looked upon as a young hero; from that time forth he was considered a sort of mysterious devil of a man. I remember that Hank Loomis, the old frontiersman, asked Sheriff Joe Crockett if he would attempt to arrest Melody singlehanded.

"Do I look like a fool?" Crockett was not ashamed to say.

And other men felt the same way about it. Even the bravest of them would not have crossed Melody, any more than they would have bared their heads and matched their agility against the flash of a thunderbolt. Because Lew was so very young, so handsome, so smiling, I think that the horror people felt for him was increased more and more. In another century he certainly would have been accused of witchcraft, and the very incident of the three Mexicans would have been enough to send him to the stake.

TWO

In the meantime, danger gathered about the head of Melody, but in a new form. I have said that he made no trouble in

9

wrong directions. Whatever were the exploits of Lew, they were performed at the expense of scoundrels who were better off the earth than on it; I have quoted already the opinion of the sheriff, and this opinion was not exaggerated, I am convinced. But the tragedy began, as you will half suspect, with the face of a pretty girl.

Lew had his hands so full of work on whatever ranch employed him, or in making his "pleasure" excursions past the danger line of Barneytown—that is to say, the old, tumbled-down district beyond the bridge, where the rascals found refuge when they arrived—that he never turned his hand to social accomplishments. He never felt the need of them until he decided to drop in at a dance in the schoolhouse one night. He had come in to watch many a dance before that, of course, but this dance was made different by the presence of Sandy Furnival.

Mr. Furnival had bought the Fitzpatrick place on the western hills which rolled up from Barney Valley. We were glad to have such a man in the community. He was not rich, but he had plenty of means. He bred good horses and was willing to buy more at a good price; he was willing to put money back into his cattle herd to improve the grade of the cows; and he looked like a solid addition to the valley. He rode in to hear a sermon of mine the first Sunday after he arrived, and he remained to talk with me about it as the others were leaving the building. He was a very blunt, down-right man who walked with a limp, due to a fall from his horse. He had a heavy, husky voice and a very terse habit of speech.

He told me briefly his name and where he lived; he told me that he was not par-ticularly interested in churches for himself or for any other man, but he thought that they were good for women, and that he had a girl whom he would make a regular member. "She's got a voice that you can use in your singing," said Mr. Furnival in his practical way, "and I'll be as much interested in your church as though I han-kered after your sermons—which I don't. By the way, that hoss shed out yonder is sort of falling down. Do you know it?"

I admitted that it was, and he told me that he would begin by putting the place in repair. And he lived up to his word. In short, he was a hard-working man who was willing to pay for what he got, and a

11

little bit more for the sake of making friends. He did not drive hard bargains and he did not expect to have people split pennies with him. On the other hand, he was as blunt as an English squire and surely there is nothing more heavy-handed. I remember calling his attention to our new altar, which was the pride of every member of the congregation.

"If that was a cow or a hoss," said Mr. Furnival, "I might be able to say something worth while your hearing; but I ain't up on fancy stuff. I'll say that it's got a sort of a fussed-up look to me."

After such an introduction to Mr. Furnival I cannot say that I looked forward to having his daughter in our choir, because I was afraid that her voice might spoil the very pleasant effect of our singing in the church. But I might have known that Furnival would not offer us a useless gift. When Mrs. Cheswick, who handled the choir for me, reported on Mary Furnival, she was in a trance of delight.

"Well?" said I.

"In the first place," said Mrs. Cheswick, "she is a dear."

"I'm so glad, Mrs. Cheswick," said I. "And her voice?"

"She has the finest, dearest pair of eyes I've ever seen," said Mrs. Cheswick, "barring those of my poor dead Theodora."

"But her voice, Mrs. Cheswick?" said I.

"And the loveliest pale-gold hair—how ridiculous that people should call her Sandy!"

I was in despair.

"The voice—the voice?" cried I, feeling that it was probably a frightful squawk.

"Oh, she sings like a bird. A real soprano—a solo voice—a perfect jewel! It will make all the rest of us seem as dark as croaking crows when you hear her open her throat!"

Mary Furnival seemed to like all men and every man; she seemed to be just as happy to talk to women, old or young, as she was to talk to adoring males. And the result was that we had our wives and our daughters as deeply in love with Sandy as the men.

Yes, that was the crowning touch, and it will help to make you understand what she was. With all her charm, and with all her beauty, and with all her wealth of grace, she was as simple as a ruled line. She could laugh at a man's joke and smile at a woman's gossip. She could stand up and sing at any one's request, and she could do a foolish Irish jig, with a great many whirls and shouts and stampings, until it convulsed a whole circle and warmed every heart to watch her. And, in seven days, she had ceased being called Miss Furnival; she was never Mary, but in a trice to the whole valley she was Sandy. Even her last name was lost! That was her charm.

Ah, well, I have looked over what I have written now about her, and I see that I have done a wretched job of it. I begin to wish that I had written more poems and fewer sermons; I have listed in my mind a thousand facts about her, but nothing will do. I am going to trust to your imaginations to help me and to assure you that no matter what picture of a girl fits most exactly into your heart, our Sandy would have fitted just as well.

I take you back from this digression to the moment when Lew Melody sauntered into the schoolroom, with men giving place to him right and left, and his gray eyes went straight across the floor to the farther corner, where Sandy sat, surrounded by her usual court, laughing and chatting and loving every moment of her life. I saw that Lew Melody saw this and turned on his

14

heel and left the schoolhouse and mounted his horse. It was the beginning of the end!

Not knowing Melody as our valley knew him, you will be surprised when you hear what he did. Any other man, having lost his heart at a single glance, would not have kept from going straight to the lady and asking her for the first vacant dance on her program, but Melody was not like others. I dare say that there was a little that was boyish and simple about him except his handsome young face and his smile. What he did was to spur his horse through Barneytown and straight across the rickety old bridge over the danger line into the Mexican section.

In the old days—which had their glory, too—Barneytown had begun as a mining town. There had been the usual rush. A hundred times as many men had come to the placer deposits as could possibly make money out of them, and the town, growing like an ugly weed, spilled across the river and down the hollow and up the hill beyond. Afterward, when men learned that there was more gold to be found in the rich black loam by plows than by picks and shovels, the population dwindled suddenly —the western quarter across the river was deserted, and the eastern half grew into a solid, prosperous little community of farmers and cattlemen from the ranches on the hills. After a time Mexican laborers began to seep up through the valley to work the farms and ride herd on the ranches, and they took up the half-wrecked shanties beyond the bridge. They repaired them enough to make them habitable; when some of them tumbled down, adobe, squat-shouldered buildings took their places, and so the Mexican quarter came to have an ugly, interesting, jumbled face of its own. When I speak of the bridge and the river as a danger line, I do not wish you to understand that the entire population consisted of villains. The vast majority of people beyond the river were honest, humble, simple, hard-working people with merry hearts and a love of festivals.

Then from the bridge, spurring his horse until the crazy old structure rocked beneath its hoofs, Melody swept up the street until he reached a house which had been built around and out of an old miner's shack, retaining the characteristics of a shack through all its growth. It was the house of the rich man of the quarter.

How far his brown hands reached up

and down the valley, with a loan here and a loan there, no one has ever known; but he was rich, even from an American viewpoint. However, these quarters were good enough for him, and in these quarters he did his business—sometimes loaning a few dollars to a laborer, sometimes loaning a few thousands to an American rancher; but I think that his lights were, after all, more Christian than those of any "gringo" bank that I have ever known.

THREE

Under the balcony, which extended above the street, Melody stopped his horse; with the butt of his revolver he banged against it, and presently the door from the balcony to the second story of the house opened.

"Who is there?" said the voice of Señora Cordoba.

Now, though Melody spoke very blunt English, as a rule, and though his Spanish was far from the purest, but mixed oddly of unbookish Mexican slang and ungrammatical sentences, yet when he spoke Spanish he scattered flowers—but always with a grin which was salt with the sweets.

"Is it you, light of my life?" said Melody to this fat señora. "Is it you, my rose, my jewel?"

"Ah, scoundrel!" said the señora, chuckling. "Ah, Señor Melody! Whose throat have you cut tonight?"

She came to the edge of the balcony and looked over the railing down to him.

"Don Luis," said she, with a shudder in her voice, "why do you come here at night? Look! There are a thousand shadows, and in the heart of every one of them there may be a knife ready for you! Come quickly into the house; come into the light!"

"My dear mother," said Don Luis, "only to see you is to be happy; only to see you is to be safe! But tell me if Juanita is with you tonight?"

"I know," said the wife of Cordoba. "Oh, cunning young liar, Don Luis! You do not come to see a fat old woman, but only because of my girl!"

"It is false!" said Melody. "It is only because she is your daughter that she is worthy of a glance. But is she in the house?"

"If a man has a diamond," said Señora Cordoba, "does he toss it out in the street, or does he keep it in a strong box?"

"I shall be with you instantly," said Melody.

He threw the reins of his horse, jumped up in the saddle, and, while the mustang flirted its heels in the air, he leaped upon the balcony and stood beside her. She looked on him half in terror and half in affection. I could never learn from Lew Melody himself what service he had rendered to the moneylender, but I half suspect that on some dark night he kept the purse, and perhaps the throat, of Cordoba from the knife of some thief. At any rate, he was free of that house, as you have seen. And he walked in with the señora like a son of the family.

It was very comfortable, inside, but quite simple—an odd mixture of Mexican-shepherd simplicity and American modernity. There were sheepskins here and there on the floor, and it was said that Cordoba himself preferred to squat on them rather than sit in a chair. There were sheepskins, too, to cover the stools and chairs with which the room was furnished, and yet, oddly out of keeping with these things, was a fine American piano in a corner of the room.

Cordoba was stretched on a couch, napping, with his hands folded on top of his fat stomach, but he wakened now and looked sleepily toward Melody, who was looking at him.

Lew Melody bowed to him. "Señor Wisdom, Señor Tranquility," said Lew Melody, "I have come to tell you that I shall give the padre the price of a mass to be said for the welfare of your soul tomorrow."

The moneylender grinned at him and pushed himself into a sitting posture.

"Welcome, Don Luis," said he. "But am I about to die?"

"I have only come for your daughter," said Melody.

"Shall I call her then?" said Señora Cordoba. "No, she has heard you. She would hear your voice through the walls of a mountain, Don Luis. And here she is coming!"

She came in at that instant, with her dark eyes shining, I have no doubt, and her dark hair combed back to show the smooth height of her forehead. Lew Melody went to her and kissed her hand.

"Silly boy!" exclaimed Juanita, delighted. Juanita was just seventeen. And she looked askance at her mother, to see if she disapproved. But Don Luis could do nothing wrong within the walls of that house.

"Look!" said Cordoba. "He is acting like a prince out of a fairy story!"

"I am the witch, then," said the señora.

"You are the fairy godmother," said Melody. "Will you let Juanita dance for me?"

"Dance? Dance?" chuckled Cordoba. "That is good! *I* shall see Juanita dance, also."

"I shall not," said Juanita, seeing that she was sure to be overruled. "I am not in the mood."

"Here," said Melody, "is a flower which has magic in it. It will make you, Juanita."

With this he broke off a rose, a full-bloomed rose, musty red, and kissed it first and then slipped it into the hair of the girl, calling to the señora: "Now, my dear señora, music, if you please! The finest music, which will run down into the slender ankles of Juanita and give them wings."

"See of what he speaks!" said Cordoba,

shaking his fat sides with laughter. "There is no modesty in this young devil!"

But here the music began. Cordoba had married above his caste a girl of many graces and some accomplishments, and among the rest she could play the piano very well. Some said that all the life of Cordoba had been spent in the making of money, not for the love of gold, but to repay his wife. But he could give her very little. She, wise woman, knowing that she had married a peasant, would not make him ridiculous by trying to lead him into the life of a gentleman. That was the reason that they had not moved to the eastern side of the river. That was the reason that they did not live in a great house at the top of the eastern hill. That was the reason that they did not have many servants— only one old woman to help with the housework. Many people attributed the poverty in which they lived to the niggardly instincts of a moneylender. But I had occasion to learn that this was not true. The life of Cordoba was for his wife, and hers was for him, and there was no home in the valley into which so much content was poured and kept as in that odd old shack across the river. And it was the great wisdom of the señora which kept it there.

In the meantime, the señora was playing, sweeping grandly and strongly into a dance theme and looking over her shoulder to watch Juanita begin, which she did a little stiffly, a little self-consciously, laughing at herself and at the gray, watchful eyes of Don Luis. But presently the rhythm reached her blood and ran through her supple young body, and tingled in her hands and in her feet until she was swaying and tossing around the big room like a leaf in a pool of wind. There was not enough for her hands to do. She snatched from the little table its chief ornament, which was a long yellow scarf with deep orange fringes, and with this she danced, making it swerve into wild, swift, graceful lines, like her own body, or letting it flutter straight behind her, as though a gale bore it up.

Melody, leaning against the wall with one arm tucked behind his head, waved a hand with half-closed eyes to keep the time with her. She ended suddenly with a stamp and an upward fling of her arms. Then she flung herself down by her father and laughed at his enthusiasm with sparkling eyes, for he was swaying back and forth, chuckling and clapping his fat hands together.

Lew Melody went and leaned over the girl.

"Sweetheart," said he, with his wicked grin, "do you not love me?"

"No!" said Juanita.

"But only a little?"

"Not this much!" said she, and whirled around on him with a snap of her fingers.

Then he added: "Can you teach me to dance as they do in a waltz and a two-step?"

Poor Juanita! Could she have known then what the guitars and the wind-hidden voices are singing over the river at this moment, and how the sweet, small sound comes to me, drowned with moonlight—but I must go slowly with this history.

"However," said Lew Melody, "if I were to give you the pinto mare which you said you liked——"

"Ah, Luis! Do you mean that?"

"She is a beggar!" cried her father, delighted nevertheless. "She is a hard trader! Oh, she is my true daughter, is she not?"

In a trice Juanita was where she wished

to be—with the hands of Luis in her hands and his eyes fixed upon her dainty feet.

"Now when you hear the beat—do you see?—ta, ta, ta! That is it! Then one step to the left, and bring up your other foot, and then again with the first foot—not too quickly. And turning—so!"

They moved slowly around the room.

"I am like a hobbled horse," said Lew Melody.

"You are not!" cried she, in enthusiasm. "You are doing it wonderfully well! Is he not, father? Is he not, mother dear—for one who has never danced before! Who could guess it? Oh, it is very well, Luis. This, then—quicker, quicker—with the beat always in your mind—see, when my finger presses on your hand—that is the beat. Look, mother, he has it already! It is wonderful, Don Luis! Now your arm around me, and with your left hand take my hand. What is the matter, Luis?"

"Is it modest?" said Melody, grinning at the señora.

"Modest?" cried she. "Oh, Don Luis, there is no modesty in these bad days! There is no modesty left, at all! Do not think of modesty, or people will call you a fool!"

"Ah, well, then!" sighed Melody, and put his arm around the girl.

"You are so pretty, Juanita, that my heart is beginning to hurry like a drum."

"Wicked Luis! Are you making love to me?"

"Is it love? I cannot tell."

"Shall I believe that?"

"Truly! I know nothing of such things. But I know that your eyes are lovely things."

"Luis!"

"Is it wrong to tell you the truth?"

"I shall not dance with you."

"Are you angry?"

"Ah, very!"

"But you are smiling, sweetheart."

She flung away from him and broke into laughter.

"Father, he is a terrible man; he is making love to me without shame!"

"Ah, villain!" said the moneylender, roaring with mirth. "I shall cut his throat!"

"One more, Juanita. This time I shall not speak a word. But you are cruel to me."

"Not another step!"

"You break my heart; besides, the pinto mare—"

"Well, I shall give you this one time to try to be good."

"If I do not talk, I shall do some terrible thing, Juanita."

"Now what do you mean?"

"I shall be in danger of kissing you, I am afraid."

"No! Even you would not dare. Now the music, mother—the beat, Luis—the beat!"

FOUR

This was not an unusual evening, from that time forth. But every night Lew Melody was at the house of the money-lender. He had quit his job on the ranch; he was making far more money playing poker, at which he was altogether too clever, and he was spending part of that money in buying clothes much more elegant than any he had ever worn before. He was so changed, and so extravagantly elegant, that if it had been any person other than he, he would have been smiled at.

In the meantime, rumor was busy; for where could rumor have found a more attractive subject than this handsome, reckless, fire-eating boy—who was now said to be paying his court to the daughter of a Mexican moneylender?

You will consider in justice to me that I did not at this time have the slightest knowledge of what was in the mind of poor young Melody concerning Sandy Furnival. All his hopes and his aspirations which turned around that girl were a blank to me, and, so far as I could tell, there was no woman in his mind except the pretty Mexican girl who lived beyond the danger line.

I said to him the first time I happened to meet him: "If I talk too frankly, you will stop me, Lew?"

"You cannot talk too frankly, sir," said Lew Melody.

"I begin with gossip that has been going around the town," said I, "concerning you and little Juanita Cordoba——"

I thought it was a beginning, but I found that it was an ending, rather. My guest leaned forward in his chair with a look, as the old poets would have said, as grim as any lion.

"There has been gossip about that?" said he.

"People will talk about anything," I said.

He answered me carefully: "You mean that two or three have been talking about this?"

"It is over the entire town," said I.

A frightful blunder, if I had known about Melody and Sandy—but how could I know? I saw, however, that I had moved Lew Melody more than I could have guessed. He merely sat back quietly in his chair, but there was enough in his face to tell me that I had cut deep.

"What does the town say?" he asked.

"That you intend to marry the Cordoba money," said I, blunter than ever.

"Do you think so?"

"I think that you go over the bridge for adventure, Lew," said I. "I don't think that you would go there to get a wife, although Juanita is a pretty girl," I added with some diplomacy.

"She is," said Melody.

"If this had happened a year or two ago," I said, "no one would have whispered about it, but in the meantime you have been growing into manhood, and growing so fast that I wonder if you yourself are aware that you are no longer a boy?"

"Perhaps I haven't thought of it," said he.

"But that is the fact," said I. "Now, my son, when we grow into manhood, the attitude of the world toward each of us changes. We may play for a certain length of time; we may amuse ourselves very much as we please so long as we are children, but as we come into manhood society begins to make demands upon us. You will be surprised if I say that people have a *right* to talk about you and your conduct from this time forth?"

Lew Melody looked at me gloomily.

"You are no longer working, but you are taking honest money of other men by your skill at cards, and while you live on that, you spend your evenings in the house of a Mexican moneylender, courting his pretty daughter. That is why people talk about you, and that is why they have a right to talk. Let me go still further. This gossip is only the warning thunder. It means that society is becoming suspicious of you. It means that the law is getting ready its great steel hand. And if you wander on in this careless, pleasure loving, idle path, and if you come to a crime—then the law will stretch out its hand toward you, and crush you, Lew—crush even you, in spite of your strength. Because the power of a hundred million men and women and children is in that hand!"

When I ended on such an ominous note, I was watching his face with the greatest care, because I was very curious to know if he would be sullen, resentful, rebellious, or simply impressed by some truth in what I had to say. I was a happy man to see that his eye remained clear. And he said to me at once: "I suppose this is in the nature of a last warning?"

"By all means, consider it such!"

He astonished me by answering: "I'm going to get work on a ranch this same day; I'm going to give up cards—and Juanita; and I'm going to start hunting for a girl to become my wife."

"My dear Lew!" said I. "I do not mean to say that all of these things should be done at once! For marriage, after all, you're rather young. I only meant this: That you ought to point in certain directions!"

"And why not get there as fast as I can?" said he.

He began to grow heated with excitement. "Oh," said he, "you must not think that I have been closing my eyes to what people think of me. They hate me, and they're afraid of me, but I want to show you and all of them that I can keep inside the law as well as the best of them! I want to show every one that I can be as straight as the best of them! Do you believe that I can do it?"

I answered him in an ill hour: "I do not! Not so long as you carry a knife or a gun on your person. Temptation will be too strong for you!"

His answer was as quick as the sound of an echo: "Then I'll never wear either a knife or a gun again!"

"Can you keep such good resolutions, Lew?" said I, bewildered by so much fire from him, and in such a right direction.

"You will have a chance to see," said he. "Today I intend to find a job, and tonight I'm going to the dance at the schoolhouse—without a gun!"

I felt—I can hardly say how!—but very like a man who scrapes a villain and finds a saint. But, of course, if I had known what Sandy meant to Lew Melody, I should have considered him a little less saintly and a good deal more human!

However, I was very soon to find out. But now Mrs. Travis came in with a tray of tea, only to find that our guest had rushed away.

"Of all things!" said she.

"Yes," said I, "you have just witnessed the end of the best day's work of my entire life!"

I write this foolish speech frankly.

Of course there had been only one reason—or one controlling reason—for those steady visits of Lew Melody to the home of Cordoba. With his characteristic thoroughness, having decided that he must not meet Sandy until he had added some social accomplishment to his list, he had spent that month arduously pursuing the study of dancing, with amazing results. Most youngsters learn to dance by stumbling about a floor a few times with some good-natured girl; then they dance at random, now and again, and confirm their faults; but Lew Melody made a profound business of it for an entire month, and on the day he left me, so filled with his new good resolutions, he was proficient, to state it mildly.

Since I knew that Lew was to be there, it was not hard for me to let Mrs. Travis persuade me to attend that dance, and accordingly we went to the schoolhouse in the middle of the evening. I did not intend to stay long because, much as I wanted to see Lew's début into society, I never felt at ease in such gatherings. Partly because the size of my dear Lydia is never more apparent than when we are dancing together, and partly beause I know that a minister's presence is always a damper on parties of young people. I do not know why it is that a minister of the gospel is supposed to possess all the disagreeable qualities of a saint and none of the good ones.

FIVE

However, when we arrived at the dance, Lew Melody was not there, and I had the privilege of seeing him enter at the very moment that I was taking Mrs. Cheswick to her seat after a dance. She did not sit down, however, but stabbed a forefinger at my ribs and whispered: "Look! If that isn't the terrible Melody

34

boy! Has he brought his Mexican girl with him?"

Which proves how very far gossip had gone in that matter, for Mrs. Cheswick was not a malicious woman. Lew Melody advanced a little from the door and stood at his ease, looking over the crowd. There was not a great deal of talking at that moment; the laughter ended as abruptly as though some one had raised a hand to hush the room. I presume that every young fellow in the schoolhouse wondered if he had offended Melody, and if that famous warrior had come for him; and every sentimental girl wondered if her beau were about to be challenged by this destroyer. Even the perspiring violinist on the musician's platform—which was where the teacher's desk ordinarily stood—stopped mopping his face and neck, to watch what Lew Melody might do next. And all other eyes were upon him. He was as cool under the pressure of those eyes as though he were the only man in the room, and all of the rest were the merest cattle. Then he saw me and came straight toward me.

When it was seen that I was his goal, it was as though a signal had been given that all was to be peace and good will, even with the terrible Lew Melody in the room; the talk and the laughter commenced again, and so there was enough noise about us for Melody to be able to speak to me without danger of being heard by others.

It was a beautiful specimen of his directness. He merely said: "I am not wearing a gun or a knife, sir; I have found a job; I have given up gambling; and now I have come to find a girl to marry me!"

He smiled as he said it, but there was enough seriousness in his manner to make me stare at him.

"Have you picked out the girl you will take, Lewis?" said I.

"I have picked out the girl I intend to marry," said he very gravely. "She is sitting in that corner—the one with the men all around her."

"Good heavens, Lew!" I exclaimed. "You don't mean Sandy Furnival?"

"Is that her name?"

"It is!"

"What's wrong with her? Is she married already?"

I could only gape on him, for it was evident that he was perfectly serious; and at that moment I saw the tragedy spread out before my prophetic eye, dimly, but a prospect filled with shadowy dangers.

So I laid a hand on the arm of Lew Melody; the stringy muscles were working a little under the tips of my fingers, and by that token I could read the excitement which he kept out of his face.

"Lewis," said I, "every young man in the valley has proposed to that girl during the past six weeks. Are you going to follow where the rest of them have made the way?"

"Is she like that?" said he. "Is she a flirt? Well, that makes no difference!"

"I don't mean that. Only consider Lewis, that——"

I could not find the fit words to continue. After all, how could I say to him: "There is the prize of the mountains, whose sweetness and whose gentleness has won all hearts. And here are you, famous for your fighting only, suspected by every one of being capable of the most frightful crimes, without a penny in the world, with a future ahead of you as dark as your past, and every prospect of leaving the woman you marry a widow in a few months— unless you change all your ways suddenly and unless the grace of the Lord wipes all thoughts of vengeance out of the minds of your thousand enemies."

I could not tell him this. I could not tell him that every one would be pleased and amused if he chose to fall in love with any other girl, but that all people would be shocked if he aspired to this charming Sandy. My own blood was a bit chilled by the prospect. And if she refused him— what then? What would his violent nature suggest to him if he fell violently in love with her and if she held him off?

All of these things were swirling through my mind.

"Be wise, Lew," said I, "and choose again."

He only said: "I want you to introduce me."

And there was nothing for me to do but to lead him toward that corner group from which half the noise of laughter went musically out across the dancing floor. When I approached, or rather when Lew Melody was seen coming close, the wall of men in front of the girl parted and fell back. And in the faces of those youngsters—brave fellows every one, I have no doubt—there came such a shadow as though this were a tiger that I led beside me. Little Sandy

Furnival stood up to shake hands with me; and so I introduced Lew Melody to her.

After that, I retired to Mrs. Cheswick and found her in a state of consternation.

"*Why* did you do that?" she asked me.

I said with some irritation: "Is the boy a monster? Is he a demon?"

"He is!" said she with much assurance. "And you know it as well as I do, Tom Travis!"

There is nothing so annoying as to have one's mind read by a woman; I felt that it would be easy to hate Mrs. Cheswick on that night. Besides, it was only a partial truth. For there were other qualities in young Melody besides his powers of destruction.

"Look!" whispered Mrs. Cheswick. "He's making a dead set at her—and—and—merciful heavens! She likes it!"

· She was not the only one that was whispering. A murmur passed ominously around the entire dance floor, and I, turning with a lump of dread in my throat, saw that she had not exaggerated. The lithe and graceful form of Melody stood over the girl like a tiger over a lamb; and the rest of her admirers had found other business which took them elsewhere. But it was not Melody who interested us most then. We could take it for granted that he would be entranced by our delightful Sandy just as every other man in the valley had worshiped her in turn. It was not that which we scanned so eagerly, but the face of Sandy herself, and there we saw what promised a sad story in the making!

We were well enough accustomed to her smiles and her pretty ways, with her eyes and her blushes and her laughter; but, upon my soul, it was not hard to see a change in her the moment she heard the voice and saw the face of Lew Melody, with the smile which he wore and the grave eyes above it. She sat quite stiff and straight in her chair, with her hands locked together in her lap and her head tilted back a little as she looked up to him. She looked like a little pupil hearing a lecture from a teacher; she looked like an enraptured child staring at a lighted Christmas tree. There was so much mingled wistfulness and pleasure in her eyes—she had grown suddenly so timid, whereas she was usually so easy and so gay, that it was not difficult for every one in that hall to see what was happening.

I told myself that it could not be true—

that the girl had too much sense and had seen too many young men before Lew ever came near her—but when the music began and they stood up to dance, I knew that the worst was upon us. They glided together around that floor like creatures which the music was not only leading, but had been made for them. Every moment we could see a new chapter of the story which was being written—first the flushed, happy face of Sandy and then the gray eyes of Lew Melody, filled with fire.

Mrs. Cheswick, at my side, uttered my own thoughts, and the thoughts of every one in the room, I have no doubt, when she said to me in a moaning voice: "What is to be done about it? Tom Travis, what is to be done about it?"

"I don't know," said I miserably. "Who could have guessed that they would both break into a flame at the same instant? It's fate, Mrs. Cheswick—it looks very much like fate!"

"Like witchcraft!" cried she, full of energy. "And if there are six real men in this valley, they'll see that Melody boy hung up by the neck on the tallest tree by Barney River before they'll allow him to carry off our poor, sweet Sandy!"

So it was Mrs. Cheswick who struck the second ominous note, and she was a prophet, also.

The dance ended, but it was not the end of Sandy and Lew Melody. They sat down together and talked and laughed in one another's eyes, and saw not another soul in the rest of the room. The group of admirers did not gather again; not a youngster came near her, for they saw the handwriting on the wall, and when the music for the next dance began, Sandy, the just and the wise and the fair, never partial in the distribution of her favors, stepped out on the floor with Melody again. By that I saw that the seal was put upon the mischief. I could not stay to watch it progress further, but I took Mrs. Travis and we started home.

SIX

Nothing else was talked of in the village, as a matter of course. Barneytown was not big enough to contain the news, but the last person whom I expected would come to bear me tidings of any affair between a pretty girl and a valley boy was Sheriff Joe Crockett. Yet I could not help thinking the better of him for it. He came in to me while I sat in my office, jabbing my pen at a piece of paper and pretending that I was making a sermon. He even forgot to take off his hat and sat down with it pushed to the back of his head, which angered me a good deal. When a man is small, as I am, there is a vast deal in the proper way of an approach. And particularly from a large fellow like Joe Crockett I like a certain measure of respect. If that wildfire, Lew Melody, would stand in the street with his hat in his hand when I addressed him, why should not the sheriff at least take off his hat when he entered my house?

Ah, well, I shall not dwell on these little things, except that the sheriff's large and lounging ways made me a bit sharp with him that morning.

He began by saying that the devil was loose, and I cannot tell what other vague and gloomy things, until I snapped out and asked him what he was talking about. At this, he considered me with a heavy frown for a long time.

"You know a good deal better than I

do, Tom Travis," said he. "You know what I mean!"

"I am too busy to waste my time guessing at trifles," said I, more pettish then ever.

"If you consider the proportions to which this affair between Sandy Furnival and Lew Melody has grown, a trifle, it is more than any one else does."

"Well, what can I do about it?"

"What we want you to do, Travis, is to go out and talk to Sandy; and if you can't talk to her, bring Furnival to time."

It was an ugly task, but some one had to undertake it. So I saddled my old gray mare and thumped up the road over the hills to the Furnival house. There I found Sandy Furnival; she answered my rap at the door, coming with a trail of song behind her. She had her sleeves rolled up—I think she was washing windows, for there was a white rag in one hand.

She wanted to know if I wished to see her father but I told her that my business was first of all with her. So she led me into the parlor and raised the shades, and offered me the rocking chair with the leather pad on it. I told her that I preferred to stand. When I am taller than the other person, I always find it better to stand; and the reverse when I am out-topped, which is usually the case, alas!

I said to Sandy: "We are worried, my dear."

"Worried?" said she. "Who?"

"The whole valley, Sandy, about you and Lew Melody."

It was half delightful and half sad to see her blush.

"I suppose that you know what I mean," said I.

She was very calm and steady about it; she looked me well in the eye and told me she understood that she must have acted very foolishly the night before, and that a great many people must be talking about her now.

"Pitying you, Sandy; but I'm glad to know that you feel it was foolishness. I suppose one touch of daylight brought you to your senses, Sandy?"

Who could have thought that there was so much blood in the girl? She grew angry at once, and asked me if I meant that as a detraction from Lew Melody. But this was too important a point for me to slide over.

I said: "Sandy, when we love you so dearly, can we be happy to see you step into such a marriage, which is bound to end in sadness?"

She did not see why it would end in sadness, and she told me so.

"If people wonder at me because I love Lew Melody," said she, "I don't care! And if they think I'm flighty for knowing in the first instant that I wanted to marry him—that makes no difference either. Only tell me why our marriage must end in sorrow."

"Because sooner or later Lew will be a fugitive from justice."

"He is going to settle down," said our Sandy. "We've talked over everything. Do you think that Lew is a sneak or a coward? No; he told me his whole story—all that I wanted to hear, at least."

She shivered a little, and I wondered how many steps Melody had described of his career in violence before she stopped him.

She said "People all stand by *expecting* him to do something wrong. Is that fair? All except you, dear Mr. Travis! And he spoke with a very warm heart about you and your kindness and your good advice!"

It brought a foolish tingle of tears to my eyes to think that he should have been praising me when I was preparing to strike at his happiness.

"Let Lew marry where he will," said I, "and I wish him the best of good fortune; but I don't want any experiments made with the heart and the soul of our Sandy."

"Ah," said she, "it is all settled. He will not even *wear* a weapon! He is working now, hard and steadily."

A dark spirit of prophecy swept over me, and I cried to Sandy: "If you'll not marry in four weeks, before that time ends I'll swear that Lew Melody will have killed another man!"

"Mr. Travis, you speak as if you hated poor Lew!"

"I speak because I love you, my dear child. And so do we all. But will you promise me that?"

"Of course, I'll promise it!" said she. "It will be too easy. Oh, I'm as sure as can be about it."

"But if he should not keep his promise—"

She looked at me in a very puzzled way. "But he has given me his word, you know," said Sandy. "And he couldn't break that! Oh, no, there's no danger at all of that!"

47

"In spite of having given you his word—what if within this month—"

"I should shut him out of my heart even if it killed me!" cried Sandy Furnival. "I should never want to see him again! I should hate him and I should scorn him!"

"Do not be too savage, Sandy," said I, "but just give me your hand on that!"

She did it, with a grip that put the strength of my own fingers to shame, and then I went out to see Mr. Furnival. I found him superintending some changes which he was making to enlarge his barn. He sat on the ridge of a low shed, with a hammer in his hand, while I stood below and told him what I had done and asked his approval.

He merely shrugged his shoulders.

"Whatever Sandy does is good enough for me," said he.

"Very well—but if Lew Melody breaks his word to her and does fight within the month, you'll help her to keep her promise to me?"

"If a double-barreled shotgun, loaded with slugs, can keep him away from her after that, I'll promise you to keep him away!" declared Mr. Furnival without heat.

When I went back to get onto my horse,

Sandy came running out to me and stopped me.

"Dear Mr. Travis," said she, "you're not like all the rest—you don't hate poor Lew?"

"No, no, no!" said I. "I want nothing more than happiness for both of you. And very few really hate him; but every one is afraid—mortally afraid of what he's apt to do. The world is like tinder, my dear, and your Lew Melody is a burning match. Do you see?"

I went back to Barneytown feeling that I had done an excellent day's work; I was so proud of myself that I spent some time finding the sheriff, and there I told him of what had happened.

But all that my fine plan in the end accomplished was the setting of a deadly trap for young Melody.

Bert Harrison, as we know well enough now, was the villain. But at that time there was not the slightest suspicion turned upon him. I must begin by saying that Bert, in the first place, was a most re-spected member of the community, be-cause he was what is called a self-made man. Any youngster who at the age of seventeen or eighteen starts out on his own resources and struggles to make a living, who discards from his soul every thought except that of money, and who plugs away at it until he has coin in the bank, a house on the hill, and a servant to open his door, is considered a leading citizen and is pointed out with pride when, as a matter of fact, he has simply coined his heart into dollars and has left everything else behind him.

Bert Harrison was this type of self-made man. He had been a simple young cowpuncher, no more virtuous than any other when he was eighteen; but at that age he had sat in, it was said, at a poker game where luck flowed his way. Some people declared that it was a little more than luck, but of this there is no proof. At any rate, he sat down poor and rose up with about ten thousand dollars in his pocket. He looked about him and bought a cattle ranch which he sold at a big profit. And so he went on buying ranches and selling again, always gaining on every deal he made. When he was thirty-two years old, he was worth a quarter of a million and certain to get the other three quarters before he was fifty.

Ordinarily one would never have taken Bert for the sort of man who would lose his head over a woman no matter how charming. But the great and the small went down before Sandy. And twice a week, on Sunday afternoons and Wednesday evenings, he rode to the Furnival house, a few miles away, to call on Sandy. If there were other callers, he contented himself with chatting with Mr. Furnival. If she were free, which sometimes happened, he would ask her to play for him, and while she played and sang, Bert Harrison sat in a stiff chair and hungered after her with a wistful smile on his lean, grim face. I suppose that he had never said three moving words to her in all the time of this odd courtship, his system was that of the slowly dropping water which is supposed to wear away the stone.

So, when the rest of the valley heard of the promise which Sandy had made to me, while all the rest nodded and grinned and said that all would turn out well in the end, Bert was the only man who rose to act. He suddenly declared that he would take a few days for a vacation—the first in fourteen years! His vacation was a railroad trip into dusty Nevada. There he got off at a little station, bought a horse, rode fifty miles across the desert to a tiny crossroads town, and asked for Stan Geary. The following evening he was in Stan Geary's shack.

I suppose that he took the precaution of leaving his pocketbook behind him, for Stan Geary was famous as a man who would cut a throat for five dollars. He had spent fifteen of his forty years in the penitentiary, and on his last trip he would have gone to the death cell had he not turned state's evidence and supplied an astonished district attorney with data that landed half a dozen rogues behind the bars.

Stan Geary's hired man—a weird little fifteen-year-old desert rat—wakened from his bed on a straw pallet in the attic, and through the trapdoor which communicated by a ladder with the room below, heard the following:

"My name is Bert Harrison. I come from the Barney Valley."

"I was jailed there once," said Stan Geary. "What might bring you up here?"

"I've got a job for you," said Bert, "if you've got the nerve to tackle it."

"If I had as much money as I got

nerve," said Geary, "I'd be sitting in a steam yacht lookin' at the pictures of my race hosses hangin' on the cabin wall. What kind of nerve do you mean?"

"Knife or gun," said Bert. "It don't make no difference which to me."

"Have a drink," said Geary. "The more you talk, the more sense I see that you got."

"I ain't a drinkin' man," said Bert honestly.

" 'Scuse me, then. Ahem! My throat gets more rawer every year, it seems to me. The time I've spent in jail sort of softens it up, I guess. Or maybe it's this alkali dust."

"Maybe," said Bert.

"All right, old son. This is the size of it: You ain't a fighting man, and you need a job done."

"In the first place, can any one hear us talk?"

"There ain't nobody in earshot, except a kid that does the chores for me, and he'd sleep through the shootin' of cannon."

"Take a look at him now and see if he ain't got an ear cocked at that trapdoor."

The desert rat was far swifter than his employer, and after Geary had climbed up, he returned to report to his guest:

"It's just the way that I said. He's snorin' his head off. I keep him busy enough to make him need no sleepin' powders at night! Take off the ropes and let 'er buck, old-timer!"

"Have you heard of a young gent that goes by the name of Lew Melody?"

"That sounds like a stage name, and I ain't no theatergoer. What might be his act? Song and dance?"

"He makes the others sing and dance, too. But they do their dancin' on the flats of their backs. He's a fightin' man, and the most of a fightin' man that ever was in Barney Valley."

"The devil!" said Geary. "That's a lie and a loud one, because I was in that valley once myself. But go on. What's this bird done?"

"Nothing but raise the devil for eight years."

"Only eight years? I ain't afraid of nobody that ain't had real experience. How old might he be?"

"Twenty-two," said Bert Harrison.

At this Geary tilted back in his chair and laughed heartily.

"Twenty-two!" said he. "Well, son, I

54

dunno that I'd take on a little odd job like that. But what might there be in it?"

"Have you a price?"

"I ain't a union man," chuckled the brutal Geary. "I've worked cheap and I've worked high. Just now I feel sort of high. I dunno——lemme see——say four or five days to get down there, and about the same to come back——and a week to look things over and do the job. That's the best part of three weeks, ain't it?"

"It is."

"And three weeks is the best part of a month, ain't it?"

"Naturally."

"Well, old son, for high-class work like this—this kid being a fightin' man, as you say—I suppose that I'd ought to be ashamed to ask less'n five hundred dollars—eh?"

"For a month's work?" said Bert Harrison.

"I'll make it four hundred," said Geary.

"Four hundred dollars, then. I agree on that. But it's the price of three good hosses."

"I know it is," said Geary, "but these ain't the old days. Take Larry Mason—that gent would bump off a puncher for a

ten-spot and then spend the ten treatin'
the gent that hired him. But them good
old days ain't no more. Things has been
runnin' downhill for a mighty long time,
ain't they?"

"I guess they have."

"Four hundred dollars, and a hundred
down."

"Come to town tomorrow and I'll give
you that hundred."

"I'll do that. You ain't startin' back so
soon?"

"I've got to start back, and start pronto."

"One drink before you go, old son."

"Nothing. I ain't used to it. So long."

"So long, then."

SEVEN

On the evening of that day, just as I
settled down behind a book and was
thanking heaven for a brief respite during
which no thoughts except the printed ones
of another man must run through my
mind—just as I was relaxing and shaking
from the tired shoulders of my brain the
load of the troubles of my parishioners
which I had borne about all the day, there

was a call to the front door, which Lydia sent me to answer because she was in the midst of the dishes. So I went, with a sigh. It might be almost anything—from a birth or a death to a sickness of body or soul, for to a humble shepherd like me the sheep blat out all their little troubles, as well as their great ones, and the doctor himself is not hurried away from his home more often than I. Also, may I be permitted to say without bitterness that he is paid for every call? Ah, well—it is not that I envy him; but on that night, as I rose from my book, I could not help wishing that I might be rewarded with even a small fee for this effort. But when I opened the front door I saw my reward as suddenly revealed to me: I saw the tonsure and the white face and the smile of Padre José!

I hurried him into my little library; I sat him down and offered him a glass of Lydia's homemade wine. He merely shook his head at me. I saw that he must be in the midst of one of his fasts—he was a little paler, a little more thin of lip and bright of eye than ever. And so, I begged him to take a little food.

"I have just dined very comfortably," said this holy liar.

Ah, Father Joseph! If he had one regret in this world, it was that he could not multiply himself into a million bodies and torment them all, doing penance and more penance, and greater penance still to redeem the sins of this wretched world.

Now there are many in my own church who disbelieve in such things, and surely I disbelieve in them also, and do not see how pain of heart and body can be pleasing to the Lord; nevertheless, whenever I was with Padre José I was overwhelmed by a sense of my own smallness and by a sense of the great heart of this man. Even now I cannot think of his goodness, his soft voice, his immense courage, without a sigh, which says to me: "Tom Travis, Tom Travis, what a petty little man you are! You could hardly have made a way in the world, except through the church; but the Padre José could have been an artist, a statesman, a warrior—but he chose to be a saint!"

In this manner I looked upon that blessed man, sorrowing over him and loving him, but with my heart full of awe. He had not reached his thirtieth year; but

I could have dropped on my knees and let him teach me the will of the Lord like a child.

"I have come to speak to you about the daughter of the moneylender, Cordoba," said he, with his usual soft voice and his usual directness. "I have come to talk about her and about a young man whom you know, if he is known at all—I mean him who is called Don Luis. The young man named Melody."

I was a little shocked by the subject which the padre suggested, but I could not say no to him. I told him to ask me what he pleased, and I admitted that we had heard a great deal of the attentions which Lew Melody had paid to Juanita.

"Every night for thirty nights," said the padre, "the young man was at the house of Cordoba, where he was already more than a son; and every night for thirty nights he told her with a smile that he loved her. Now, my brother, this girl is seventeen, but at seventeen a girl cannot jest too long concerning love; the very word has a power over her; it is an incantation. She taught him to dance, do you see?"

When he said that I saw a great deal, for my eyes were suddenly opened to the

59

craft of this strange young man who was able to plan so far ahead and work so patiently all the time. At the very moment when I had talked with him so seriously about the attentions which he was paying to the Mexican girl, the rascal had not the slightest seriousness of intention toward her. I could see that now, and I felt that I had played a good deal the fool in this matter. However, be that as it might, I had to confess the truth to Padre José.

I merely said: "Dear father, I will confess to you that I love this young man in spite of his faults, which are very many. I think that he spent that entire month learning to dance so that he could appear in a more favorable light before another girl—one of his own people."

The face of the good padre withered with pain. He stood up at once, saying: "Ah, well, it is not the first time that I have had to carry sad tidings. God forgive him. Since you love him, I shall pray for him; but where is there such cruelty as that of man to woman, my brother? What my poor girl has heard of Don Luis and Miss Furnival is true?"

I could only nod, and the padre left me and walked out into the night. I could not help thinking then, with a little more humility than is generally granted to me, that if Lew Melody had had such a spiritual adviser as Father Joseph, his life might have been changed.

The next morning, black destiny took a hand in this history again. It happened that on this day the rancher for whom Lew Melody was working sent him to town with two empty wagons and eight mules on a jerkline to haul out several tons of baled hay; and on that same morning Stan Geary arrived in town just in time to saunter down the street as Lew drove past, singing out to his mules, and checking them deftly down the street to avoid the chuck holes.

All that Geary knew of the appearance of Lew was a description which he had picked up the day before while he was in the neighborhood, but a child of three could have described Melody unmistakably, his eyes were so solemn and his smile so constant. So Geary knew him as well as if they had been old acquaintances.

I have often wondered why the butcher did not simply snatch out a revolver on the spot and send a bullet through the head of Lew; there could have been no resistance, for it was afterward known that Lew, according to his promise, did not carry a weapon. However, a man never seems so feeble as when he is poised on a high seat of a wagon with a bulky team stretched out by spans ahead and a pair of coupled trucks rolling behind. I suppose that Geary, staring up to the youngster as the seat rocked back and forth while the wagon rumbled over the rough street, told himself that he might as well do his work in a way which he always preferred—with his bare hands.

"How about a ride?" he sang out, and without waiting for an answer, since he had a monkey's agility in spite of his bulk, he swung himself up to the lofty seat and stowed himself at the side of Lew Melody.

No one knows exactly what passed between them; I can imagine the great beast leering at Melody with a swinish and terrible hunger in his bright little eyes. At any rate, before that wagon had rattled on for a half a block the two had gripped one another. The little son of Mrs. Graham saw everything. He told afterward that Geary had grappled with Lew Melody, and how, after a few seconds of struggle the one aim of Geary seemed to be to disentangle himself from his battle rather than continue with it. It was like trying to disengage himself from the claws of a panther, however, and in Geary's fury and astonishment and terror he flung himself blindly off the seat and carried Melody with him to the ground. That shock would have half killed normal men; it merely served to untangle this pair of warriors. The youngster saw them roll to their feet and watched Melody leap in at the big man through the cloud of dust which they had raised.

He declares that he saw the flash of steel in the hand of Geary, but whether it were knife or gun, it was not used, for as it appeared the driving fist of Lew Melody smashed home against the face of the monster. There was no resisting that blow. It struck the bridge of Geary's nose and flattened it against his brute face as though a swinging sledge hammer had thudded home there. The weight of the stroke knocked Geary fairly from his feet and plunged him into a pool of liquid white dust.

The mules, in the meantime, had taken the first symbol of trouble as an excellent opportunity to rest; Melody now climbed back to his seat and drove on toward the warehouse, leaving Geary behind him. Only the Graham boy saw the giant lurch up out of the dirt, his nose closed and his breath drawn through his gaping mouth. He looked wildly around him for a moment, and then started rapidly back up the street.

No matter how stunned he was, I presume that he understood the town would not be safe for him if the sheriff heard of this last transgression. He took his horse and left at once for the road over the eastern hills of the valley—in other words, toward the Furnival ranch, because he had heard by this time of the affair between Lew and Sandy.

As for Lew Melody, he came to find me as soon as his load was stowed on his wagons. He told me everything that had happened, and he swore to me that he had not provoked the attack.

"I thought that he was drunk," said Lew, "except that there was no whisky on his breath. He went at me like a crazy man, and I had to fight back. Will this go against me, sir?"

But I, having heard so much of Geary, felt that there was nothing wonderful in this affair except that a man so much

64

smaller than the monster had tamed Geary with his bare hands. Of course, I assured Lew that he deserved nothing but praise; but again I begged him to be careful.

EIGHT

It turns me sick even now when I conceive the intoxicating malice which must have been pouring through the soul of Stan Geary as he rode out of Barneytown on the eastern road. Two or three people saw him go in that direction, but they did not connect it, naturally, with the Furnival place. If the word had been carried to me, I think that I should have put two and two together and guessed that the direction in which Geary rode had something to do with an attack upon Lew Melody. However, no word was brought to me. For once my system of gossiped news failed to function.

The intention of Geary, beyond any doubt, was to secrete himself near to the Furnival house and wait for the next chance visit that his quarry paid to the lady of his heart. Nothing could have been simpler, nothing could have been more delightful than this, from his viewpoint. Having experienced the deadly grip of Lew's hands in actual combat, having been crushed and subdued by one man for the first time in his life, there is no doubt that he would not risk a fair fight with guns thereafter. What he planned was murder as secret and safe as the exploit of any scalp-taking Indian.

At any rate, he lurked near the house the rest of the day. Perhaps he may have seen, in the distance, the winding dust cloud which the laboring wagons of Lew left in the air as the mules tugged up the long slope toward the ranch where he was working. But if he recognized the wagons, he was not tempted to make his attack on the open road again; perhaps the very sight of the wagons made him feel that they were bad luck for him. However that may be, he remained in covert until the falling of the dusk, when Sandy Furnival, bound home in haste, cantered her horse across the hills toward her father's house, singing as she came.

The men in the bunkhouse heard the sweet, sharp sound of her voice and hushed their own chatter to listen to it; they heard the voice stop abruptly, and when they went to spy out the matter, they saw that she had stopped her horse and that she was conversing with a huge shadow of a man on a huge horse. By that dull light they could make out no more.

Presently Sandy broke away from the man and came hurrying toward the house, and past it to the bunkhouse. There was no song in her face as she stopped before the punchers. She asked them if any of them had seen a giant with a smashed face, and who he was—and how he had dared to stop her.

She got no further than that. That any one in the world should have dared to stop their darling Sandy was an incredible insult to those fiery cowhands. They shot into saddles and ripped through the dull light of the evening, guns ready in their hands. However, the beast was gone.

He gave her enough of a shock, however, to make her break out with the whole story the moment that she saw Lew Melody, when he galloped over to see her that night. She did not quite finish, for before the end Melody had run to a gun rack in the corner of the hall and caught up a revolver and opened it to make sure that it was loaded. Then he started for the door.

She saw what she had done, then, of course. She threw herself in front of him and begged him to stop. He merely brushed her aside; but then she stopped him again with her mere voice and made Lew Melody, with all the devil that was burning in him, turn back to face her. I can see our Sandy as she must have been, and I can hear the agony and the grief and the dread and the horror in her voice, when she said to him: "If you go out, you'll find him; and if you find him, you'll fight; and if you fight, you'll break your word to all of us. Lew, there are only twenty days left!"

Old Furnival, sitting in the corner, saying never a word, waited and watched and lifted neither voice nor hand to influence young Melody. I suppose there was enough in the gray eyes of Lew to keep the rancher dumb; and I suppose that it was at that moment that he made up his mind that this man could not be the husband of Sandy.

He saw Melody raise a hand to shut out the accusing face of the girl, and heard Melody muttering: "I've got to go; I've got to find him, Sandy!"

It made her frantic; she caught at his

hand and dragged it down and made him look at her.

"If you do it, you'll lose me!" she cried to him. "Do you understand? If you break your word like a rotten rope, I'll keep mine. I'll never see you again; I'll never speak your name! Lew, for God's sake, stay with me and I'll help you fight it out!"

He wavered, then; but I suppose that he heard her only dimly. For, as much as he loved her, the instinct was still too fresh and strong in him. He had fought once before that day, and his hands and his heart must have been tingling with the battle. It is the taste of whisky in the throat of the drunkard that drives him on to call for yet another drink—that wakens him at night, half mad with a ravening thirst, and sends him stumbling out into the dark. So the tiger in Melody thrust the lover aside. He did not try to argue with her; he simply turned on his heel and fled out into the moonlight.

In the hollow behind the barn and the sheds, the men of the bunkhouse heard the sudden chattering of guns and rushed out to see what had happened. They did not need lanterns; the moon was so bright that it showed them, under the thick pattern of the shadow of the oak tree, the huge, outstretched body of Geary. How he appeared I have no wish to know except that it was found that a bullet had struck him fairly between the eyes.

I suppose that when the bullet was fired, and when that mighty hulk of a man fell forward on his battered face, the passion died out of poor Lew Melody as the life died out of his enemy. Yet he must have wandered through the hills, cursing his fate, wondering what demon haunted him, for a full hour. It was that length of time before he came once more to the house of Furnival.

I suppose that that grim old chap recognized the light, quick, stealthy tread of the killer as Melody came up on the veranda, for when he opened the door to the knock of Lew, Furnival had a sawed-off shotgun tucked under his arm, with a forefinger curled about the triggers. There was enough lead in that weapon to have washed the life out of ten strong men, and Furnival was quite prepared to use it all in one terrible blast against Melody.

But I suppose that a child could have controlled poor Lew Melody, after the fire had burned out in him. He leaned against the side of the door with a fallen head and a sick face, and when he saw Furnival with the ready gun he rubbed his hands across his eyes and looked again to make sure that he saw aright.

"I've come back to beg for one more chance," said Melody, pleading for the first time in his life.

"You've had your chance," said Furnival. "You get no more out of me."

"May I speak two words to Sandy?" said Melody.

"You may not," said Furnival, with his finger more stiffly pressed against the triggers. "It's time for you and me to say so long, Melody."

"Let me hear it out of her own mouth," groaned Lew. "I'll make no trouble, I swear it!"

Furnival turned his idea in his mind for a moment and then he called out, without taking his eyes from Melody: "Sandy, here he is. Will you talk to him?"

And the voice of Sandy came back, as cold and as clear as a bell—because sorrow will make a strong soul stronger and harder: "I've told him what it would mean to me, and I haven't changed my mind."

71

"I guess you hear her talk," said Furnival.

"Mr. Furnival," said Lew Melody—though to me, who knew him so well, it seems incredible that he could have begged so—"let me have six months while things settle down. Then let me come back and see her!"

Perhaps I have shown you Furnival as a matter-of-fact man; he was a grim man, also, and now he said: "I've seen your dead man, down under the oak. Well, Melody, I'd as soon have seen her married to him as to you."

And he struck the door shut in the face of Lew.

NINE

Furnival was not a talkative man, and, of course, Sandy and Lew Melody would never have spoken a syllable concerning what had happened, but such news could not be hidden. It was known, not only that young Melody had killed a man and broken his word to the Furnivals, but, also, every painful detail of the manner in which he had been refused the Furnival house after the crime was noised abroad and repeated with many decorations. Even the stalest imagination was able to think of a few ornaments for such a moving tale. I had to listen to at least twenty variants upon the truth before the sheriff called on me the next morning.

He gave me the confirmation of all the important points. And my miserable reflection when he had ended was simply: "We've crucified Melody, but if it saves Sandy from him it's worth while, I suppose. And yet there's something horrible, Crockett, in persecuting a man who had rid the world of such a vile rascal as that Geary!"

The sheriff said with violence: "They had ought to give Lew Melody a medal in gold with what he's done wrote down in gold across the face of it. I dunno that you and me, Travis, in our whole lives will ever do as much good in the world as this here boy has done in bumping off Stan Geary."

You will see by this that the sheriff was in the mood for using superlatives.

"Will he be quiet, do you think, when I go out to arrest him?"

It staggered me. It popped me out of

73

my chair and popped me back again with a groan.

"Arrest him, sheriff?"

He nodded.

"But," cried I, "what has he done that's worthy of arrest? Haven't you told me yourself that what he should have is a gold medal?"

"It ain't what he ought to get—not in the eyes of you and me and folks with sense. It's what the public wants, and the public wants to see him arrested!"

But the sheriff went on: "I set up to have some sense, but I don't set up to have more sense than most folks. What the majority wants, that's what I'm here to do. Sometimes, maybe, they'd be wrong— like this case. But mostly they be right. When I know what they want, I shut my eyes and I go ahead and do it. I'm the servant of the county, Travis, and don't you never forget it; and if the county said to me, 'Go arrest Tom Travis,' I'd go and do it quicker'n a wink!"

It was very uncomfortable logic, and I told him so.

He merely said: "The main thing is will this fool kid let me arrest him?"

"Certainly," said I, "because he knows

perfectly well that after he's arrested he'll very quickly be turned loose. But at any rate you'll take several men with you to make that arrest?"

"I'd like to," sighed Joe Crockett. "Lord, how I hanker to take out three or four of the boys that are handy with their guns and don't make no fuss about usin' 'em! But it can't be done!"

I was amazed and asked him why it could not be done.

"Because I'm the sheriff of this here county," said Joe Crockett. "Right now I wish that I'd never seen the job. But I've never been afraid to go out and arrest one man all by himself, and I ain't goin' to start now. Not at my age. My habits are all fixed and settled on me."

I confess that it made the hair stand up on my head, and I told him so, but the sheriff's mind was indeed fixed. He bade me farewell and left, but very slowly. I never saw a man take so long in settling his hat upon his head or in opening and passing through the front door, or in arranging his stirrups, or in untethering his horse, or in dragging himself wearily into the saddle. A child could have guessed what was passing in his mind: and I was sick at heart—for Sandy, for Lew Melody, and for poor Sheriff Joe Crockett.

At noon, Melody rode in from the fence line, and he found Joe Crockett waiting for him, sitting on one end of the watering trough and whittling at a stick with his hat pushed far back on his head to shade his neck as he slouched forward. The first impulse of Melody was the right one, for he reined in his horse at the first glimpse of the man of the law. But after an instant of thought he seemed to decide that his suspicion could not be right. He went on and spoke to the sheriff as he dismounted and jerked the bridle from the head of his pony so that it could drink.

So that historic conversation began.

"How's things, Lew?" said the sheriff.

"Fair," said Melody. "How's things with you?"

"I've got a stitch of lumbago that's fetchin' me up pretty short," said Crockett. "That's a sign that I'm gettin' on."

"You ought to go to bed, then. Old Man Simmons is bothered a lot that way. He always goes to bed and beats it pretty quick."

"Simmons ain't the sheriff," said Crockett.

"Business keeps you stirring?"

"That's right."

"What sort of business brings you out this way?" asked Melody with a twinge of suspicion.

"Well," said Crockett, "there's a lot of things. I might be out this way to cut for sign of that cattle-killing grizzly. I ain't above hunting bear for the good of the county. Then there's old Charring. I got to talk to him about where that rascal of a son of his might of disappeared to. You see, there's always something to do. Besides," he added, "there's the case of that skunk, Geary, that you bumped off last night."

You will say that this approach was about as diplomatic as any you can imagine; and yet Lew Melody was too highly strung to miss the first taint of suspicion in the air.

"And what about Geary?" he asked. "Do I get a pension from the county for that good job?"

The sheriff cast away the stick which he was whittling and began to make a cigarette.

"Well," said he, "what spoils the pension idea is that Geary wasn't wanted for nothing particular."

"I might of brought him up for assault and battery," said Lew Melody. "He jumped me for nothing in the town, yesterday morning."

"I've heard tell about that, which you thumped him pretty bad for what he tried, they say."

"I did what I could," answered Melody, grinning.

"But the main trouble about this thing," went on the sheriff, "is the fact that there ain't no charges agin' old Geary at all—not just right now. He was all cleared off and wiped up clean by turning state's evidence—the dog! So in the eyes of the law he's just the same as a newborn babe, pretty near."

"Look here," broke in Melody, "the chief business that brought you out here was on account of me and Geary. Is that right?"

"I ain't saying that it ain't the most important thing."

"What was wrong?" asked Melody. "It was a fair, stand-up fight—except that he started it by trying to pot me from behind a tree."

"Might you have any proof of that?"

"Sure. This!"

He took off his hat. The crown, toward the peaked top of the sombrero, was nearly punctured by a half-inch hole.

"This will save me from having air holes punched," said Lew Melody.

"Well, some folks might say that that hole was shot into the hat afterward."

"Some might," admitted Lew with a frown.

"And then, again—what might make some talk was the way that you started out rampaging after him."

"Crockett," said Melody, growing more and more excited as he saw the case against him turning black, "you know as well as I do that the fight was fair!"

"Oh, sure I do, Melody. But it ain't what I think; it's what other folks suspect. And the best way is always to clear up all of the suspicions."

"I suppose that's right, but what are the suspicions now? And who ever asked me questions like this or held me on such a short rope before? It isn't the first time that I've dropped a man, is it?"

"Not the first," said the sheriff. "No, that's one bad side of it—about the worst side. Folks know that you've been a killer since you was a kid. But every gent that you ever dropped before happened to be one that was on the wrong side of the book. It was always somebody that was wanted, and that was wanted bad. Most of them that travel transient through the west side of Barneytown are that sort, you know! But this time it's a man that the law ain't got a thing against—technically. And then there's the other part of it. Couldn't be said that this here fight was an accident, because there's folks that seen you grab a gun and run for the outdoors to get at him, even after you was stopped and argued with. Well, Melody, you see how the case sizes up!"

Lew Melody dropped his hands on his hips and stared down at the sheriff for a long moment.

"Is that the way that you see it?" said he.

"Me? It ain't what *I* see. And it ain't what the judge'll see. And it ain't what the jury'll see. But it's best all around for you. to go in with me and stand your trial, and the whole thing will be dropped and never thought of afterward."

I know that the diplomacy of the sheriff has always been much celebrated because of the skillful manner in which he handled this affair, but I confess that I have always felt he laid an undue emphasis upon the case which the law might bring against Lew Melody. He wished with all his might to explain to Lew that he had a cause for arresting him; he succeeded so well that, before he finished, Lew was convinced that the state had a case against him good enough to land him in the penitentiary. I have heard that had it been a straight, unadulterated matter of trial for murder with a death penalty involved, Lew would have gone in and faced the music. But what he saw in this affair was not a death penalty, but the dreadful darkness of a long prison term closing over the prime of his life.

"So," said the sheriff, "that's why I've come out to ask you into town with me, Lew."

He said it very cheerfully, but Lew had heard too many reasons before this.

"I'm to go to Barneytown," said Lew, "and be tried by a jury of men who've known me for a troublemaker all the days of my life. They're going to try me for murder of a man with no crime charged against him right now. What do you think that my lot would be?"

"Why, Lew, you'd be acquitted, of course. I'd give you my rock-bottom word on that!"

Melody shrugged his shoulders. "Every man can make a mistake," said he, "and I've an idea that this is your mistake, Crockett. No, I'm sorry to say that I'm not going in!"

Crockett digested this remark with a wry face. And that face grew several shades lighter.

"You won't do it, Lew?" he repeated.

"I won't do it! Bah! Don't I know that they'd railroad me if they had half a chance?"

The sheriff stood up slowly. "I want to make it plain to you, Lew, that I'm askin' you mighty polite to go to town with me. I ain't suggestin' no irons on your wrists. Nope, I'll go you better than that. I'm simply arrestin' you in the name of the law and askin' you to report at the jail—some time today. I'm askin' you to promise to do that!"

An odd manner of making an arrest, you will say; but the courage of the sheriff had been proved a hundred times; he could afford to use novel methods.

"I know that you're a white man, Crockett," said Lew Melody. "I've always tried to keep from stepping on your toes."

"I know you have, Lew," said the sheriff gently.

"I respect you, Crockett, and I like you a lot; and I appreciate a lot the way you've showed me all the sides of this thing, but I'm not—"

"Wait a minute, Lew! For God's sake, remember that if you say no, I've got to try to *make* you come with me!"

"I tell you, Crockett, I want no trouble with you. Give me a half a minute to get away from you and then catch me if you can. But don't try to put the irons on me by force! Because you can't do it!"

"Lew," said Joe Crockett, "I know that I can't. I know that you're fast and a better shot than me, and a stronger and quicker man and a better fighter every way from Sunday—but I'm going to take you to Barneytown or die tryin'!"

I cannot think of it without growing weak—those two honest-hearted fighting men, standing face to face with nothing but the greatest respect and gentleness in their souls for one another, and yet forced to go on from one dangerous word to another until nothing remained except a gun play.

Melody was greatly moved. It is said that he turned perfectly white and begged Crockett with a trembling voice not to go any further in the matter.

For answer, poor Crockett took the handcuffs out of his pocket.

"I've served this county too many years," said he, "to be afraid of dyin' for it now. Lew Melody, I arrest you in the name of the law. Hold out your wrists for me!"

Melody stepped lightly back.

"Then take what's coming to you!" shouted Crockett, and he snatched at his gun.

You will understand that he was a famous warrior himself; but yet he was so slow in comparison with Lew that the youngster had time to select a special target, and that was what saved the life of Crockett. For, instead of aiming at a vital spot, Melody had time to pick a less fatal target. He merely shot Crockett through the shoulder, and the gun of the sheriff dropped to the ground.

TEN

People who have never seen a bullet fired into a human body have strange ideas about it; and, as a rule, they seem to think that the lead whisks through flesh as smoothly as a knife thrust. But I have seen a two-hundred-pound man knocked flat on his face by the impact of a big, blunt-nosed .45 caliber slug from a long-barreled Colt, which shoots with almost the driving force of a rifle. And what the slug meets it usually tears or breaks in a shocking manner. But the bullet which Lew Melody sent through the body of the sheriff was so neatly placed that it went through the shoulder without smashing a single bone; yet the force of it twisted Joe Crockett around and made him slump against the watering trough. He would have fallen to the ground, had not Melody caught him in his sinewy arms.

There the sheriff lay, gasping with agony, as he saw the men running toward him from the bunkhouse.

"Lew," said he to Melody, "for heaven's sake don't run away from them. Let them take you, and I'll never appear to press a charge for resisting arrest. Don't run, Lew! Stand fast, and——"

It was about as honest and as kind a thing as any man of the law had ever said, I think, and particularly a Western sheriff with a bullet newly through his body from the hand of a criminal he had tried to arrest. But while he was speaking the men from the bunkhouse, who had seen every happening in this affair, and who had heard part of it, were coming with a rush. They had been gathered together, washing up for noon dinner, and now they came in a compact group. Joe Crockett told me afterward that he thought Lew would have taken his advice, even in that crisis, had it not been that some of the punchers were already drawing their guns as they ran. They had a foolish impression that, instead of supporting a wounded man, Melody, with fiendish cruelty, was murdering a helpless man! They were ready to shoot, and they did start shooting, in fact, as soon as he allowed the body of Crockett to slip gently to the ground.

It left nothing for Lew Melody to do

except to flee, unless he wished to stay and slaughter the whole crew of them. As perhaps he could have done, for they were a wretched lot of marksmen, as Crockett avouched later. Indeed, the average marksmanship of cowpunchers with revolvers is strangely bad. I have gone into a saloon after seven or eight score bullets from revolvers were fired at point-blank range—result: windows, doors, floors, and ceilings and glassware smashed all to bits; but in human casualties not more than one dead and two or three slightly wounded! One would think that even accident would cause a greater damage.

However, Lew did not pause to consider this. The moment the sheriff was out of his arms, he heard the bullets whizzing around him and he knew that he must run for his life. It was then that he made a decision which was both wise and foolish. It was wise because his own horse, which he had just ridden in off the range, was a rather tired and very commonplace cow pony, whereas the sheriff's horse was a handsome bay with a thoroughbred's stride and something of thoroughbred blood in it, also. But it was very foolish even in that emergency for Lew to steal that same strong bay horse. It might save him for the moment, but it made him something just a whit more detestable than a confessed murderer: a horse thief!

However, he was in the saddle and away in the split part of a second. He was a natural horseman; in a trice he had gathered that fine animal under him and pushed it to full speed. Another second or two and he had swerved out of view behind the corner of the nearest shed.

They had sight of him after that, as they pursued, but with such a running start, and on such an animal, there was never a chance for them to capture him, unless he foolishly doubled back straight into their arms. In an hour he was out of hearing and out of sight, and though they thrashed about the countryside all the rest of that day, with some score or two of other riders to help them out, they did not come upon any traces of the fugitive. He had wisely faded away toward the north, and toward the north the pursuit headed, while calls came back to us in Barneytown to make the telegraph buzz with the news and to carry the word to every little town on the line north and east and west of the valley. For somewhere in that direction was riding the criminal who had resisted arrest under the charge of murder, and who had shot down the famous sheriff, Joe Crockett.

It was spectacular tidings, and many and many a stalwart warrior of the cattle ranges, and many a shrewd, brown-faced farmer from the valleys, oiled his rifle and cleaned it and mounted his horse and struck in with some company of his fellows to haunt the probable paths by which Lew Melody might flee.

But what seemed most odd to every one after the event was that no one had considered for an instant the trail which Lew did finally adopt, and that was the back trail down the eastern ridge of the hills and straight to the ranch and to the house of Furnival!

Yes, for there he went after the dark had fallen, and cached his horse in a stout thicket near the front of the rambling old house. Then he slipped up to the dwelling and climbed to the second story. A moment later and he was through the window and crouched in a corner of Sandy's room.

She went upstairs early that night—as soon as the after-dinner dishes were finished. She went upstairs, poor child, to shed some of the tears which she had been striving to keep from showing since the news of this second crime of her lover's had come to her. And, I suppose, she would have tried to moan away some of her despair.

But the instant she turned up the flame of the lamp she carried and settled it on the table, she saw a tall shadow standing in a corner of the room, and shrank with a little gasp from Lew Melody.

I suppose that neither of those two wretched young people thought of it, at the time, but there was something childish in his desperate approach to her. He dropped on his knees in front of Sandy and reached for her hands and drew them down.

"Sandy, Sandy, Sandy dear!" said Lew Melody. "I'm not trying to get you to talk to me, after you swore you never would. But I had to give myself one last sight of you before I started out."

What did Sandy do? She drew him to his feet and made him sit down in a chair, and she leaned behind that chair, with her breath beside his face, as she whispered: "Where are you going, Lew?"

"Outside the law," said Lew Melody.

"If you do that, you'll never come back."

"I'll never come back," said he.

"Ah, my dear!" said she, and she began to cry. "But can't you come back and take your chance? I know that they can't harm you for—the Geary man. And the sheriff is not badly wounded."

"I'm a horse thief," said Lew Melody, and that word was enough for both their Western minds until she cried to him: "But if the sheriff didn't really press that charge—and he wouldn't——"

"What would I gain by it?" asked Lew Melody. "Sandy, could I come to you, if I won through all the danger of it?"

"No, no," said poor Sandy. "My father is a strange man, Lew. And now that he's made up his mind about you, you would have to kill him before you could have me. But beyond that, I've given an oath, Lew. Oh, what have I done that God should wish to torture me so?"

"You'll forget me in a month, Sandy," said he. "Because inside of that month I'll have done enough things to make you wish that you'd never seen me!"

"Do you say that?" said Sandy. "But I know, I've always guessed, that you could

91

be terrible, but you could never be cruel or really wicked and low. I know that, Lewis!"

The devil made Mr. Furnival miss his newspaper, and he came to the foot of the stairs to call Sandy.

"Will you kiss me once before you go down?" said Melody.

"I cannot," said she.

"It's the last time, Sandy. I'll never have to ask you again."

"I cannot," said poor Sandy.

And then she hurried down the stairs and to her father.

As for Lew Melody, he stood there in the yellow of the lamplight, drinking in every bit of that room feverishly, hungrily. Whatever he saw was a part of her. That chair she sat in; the mark in that book her fingers had placed there. Before that mirror she had stood and looked at herself before she went out on that very night which first gave her a sight of him.

He pressed his hands across his eyes and prayed that he should not go mad; and so he slipped out the window as he had come, and down softly to the ground below, and so to the thicket of trees where he had left his horse, and then away on the strong-striding bay. This time to the north.

He stopped at the crest of the next hill. He could mark the house clearly and the light of every window, and while he sat in the saddle there, waiting; like a signal to him he saw the window of her room go black, and by that he knew that she had come back and blown out the light to sit alone in the dark with her grief, because she could not bear the sight of the familiar things around her.

"It's the black signal," he said to himself grimly. "It means that it's time for me to be off while she—" and he drew a hand across his eyes.

Then Melody turned his face to the north and jogged steadily away.

ELEVEN

When the desert rat lay coiled on his straw pallet in the attic of the shack of Stan Geary and listened to the short and pleasant debate between his master and Bert Harrison, and when he gathered from that debate that Geary's services were being purchased for the killing of a man, the rat was not shocked. He had bits of conscience left to him, but they were scattered here and there and not readily available. He remained, to the very end, the strangest morsel of humanity that it has ever been my fortune to encounter; and I think that if the rat thought very much about the journey of his master south to the Barney Valley, it was with rather a pleasant anticipation of the end that was to be. He himself had felt the heavy hand of Geary so often, and those cruel fingers had so wrung and crushed his body, that the rat was glad to think that the mighty hands would be used upon another creature.

He prepared, in the meantime, to wait for the return and enjoy the absence of Geary. How long his master would be away, the rat could not tell. Geary had said: "A week!" But that might mean anything from a day to a month or more. In the meantime, Geary in leaving had tossed the youngster a dollar and told him to spend that present with care!

But it was indeed a present to the rat. He had no intention of spending a single cent out of the hundred. For what did he need to sustain his life? There was Geary's old rifle in the corner, and an ample supply of powder and lead and shells. With those materials he could turn out bullets which were a delight to the eye, and Geary professionally and habitually preferred the handiwork of the boy to store bullets out of a machine.

"They got a sort of a nose to foller the right trail, the bullets that kid turns out!" Stan Geary was fond of saying.

So with that rifle and with those bullets of his own manufacture, with a little cornmeal, baking powder, sugar, and salt, the youngster was prepared to face a stay of any length whatever, in the desert. For he was a wonderfully skillful hunter—that is to say, he was a wonderfully patient one. Geary had not taught him; Geary could not teach him; instead, he was the provider of the food for the table as well as the cook and the dishwasher.

A week, and then two weeks passed; but Slim was not alarmed. He was very much contented to remain there alone for an indefinite period. He was fourteen, now. His body was lithe and hard muscled. He was not large, but he was as tough as whip leather. And in the hardships of the desert he found his recreations!

Then a stranger from the direction of town—Slim knew that direction, though Geary had never let him go to the place—came over the low, sandy hills under a blistering sun and drew rein at the door of the shack. Through that open door, without dismounting, he could see Slim sitting cross-legged on the floor, deftly sewing together rabbits' skins which he had dressed himself. The skin of the rabbit is not tough, but it possesses a soft and comfortable warmth, and all the long summer, Slim was busy preparing himself against the ardors of the winter—laying up stores of dried or smoked meat, and laying up warm furs, and mining the long roots of the mesquite for fuel. The stranger looked in and wondered at this boy, more than half naked, and brown as a Mexican.

"Hello, kid," said he.

Slim did not reply; he merely made a covert gesture to bring the knife which lay on the floor, closer beside him.

"Are you deaf?" asked the traveler.

Slim, since his back was turned, could afford to smile with satisfaction. He was not yet able to wreak his vengeance upon huge Stan Geary, but in the meantime it was no little satisfaction to annoy all other men in large ways or small ones.

The rider was sufficiently irritated and interested to dismount from his horse and step through the doorway. There he looked around upon the frightful poverty of that wretched shack. It was literally falling to pieces. The leaning, staggering walls had been braced up by the boy through a sort of clumsy masonry—rocks being built up in the corners to support the flimsy walls against the shock of the winds. And, to keep the walls themselves from disintegrating, because he had no nails, the boy had fastened the boards together with thongs of leather. The floor itself was bare. There had once been a boarding across it; but that boarding had been torn up by Stan Geary in an idle moment and thrust into the stove to make one winter's day cheerful.

The rider was one who had known poverty all of his days, but he had never seen a white man living in such conditions as these.

"Might your pa be around?" he asked.

Slim turned his head over his naked

shoulder and regarded the other with a baleful calm.

"I've got no pa," said the boy. It must have startled the other a little.

"You live here all alone!" the stranger exclaimed.

"Did I say that? I didn't! Stan Geary, he hangs out here a part of the time."

"Stan Geary!" cried the puncher.

"Yes," said the savage boy, "and if he heard you yap like that when you was namin' him, he'd bust you in two till the stuffings ran out of you!"

"Kid," said the good-natured puncher, "maybe Geary has stood by you and done you some good turns—and maybe again the turns he's done you ain't been as good as you think. Anyway, you better pack up your things and come along with me. I see that you got a pony pack yonder; and there's a saddle—"

"What the devil are you talkin' about?" said the boy.

"Geary is dead," said the puncher gently.

It had an astonishing effect upon Slim. He struck his hands together in a great fury.

"You lie!" he yelled at the puncher. "It

ain't true. Because he's gonna be saved for me—and I'm gonna—he ain't dead! He can't be dead, and stole away from me!"

The cowpuncher made out vaguely that this unusual boy was lamenting not the sudden departure of Stan Geary from this world, but the bitter loss of an opportunity which he had himself long looked forward to. He merely groaned because the slaying of Geary had been stolen from his own hands!

The desert rat grew more calm after this. His next question concerned the slayer of the man who had tormented him so long.

"It's the only man in the world that *could* have killed Stan Geary, I guess," said the cowpuncher. "It's Lew Melody, of Barney Valley. He's gone north—they ain't found his trail yet. And they've planked out a pretty neat reward for him, dead or alive."

"Hey?" cried Slim. "Reward? Reward on him for what?"

"Why, nothing but murder, hoss-stealin', resistin' arrest, and shootin' the sheriff and woundin' him. That's all he's done lately that's worth talkin' about."

"Murder of who?" asked the boy in the same sharp tone.

"Of Stan Geary, of course. I've just finished tellin' you that. Now, kid, d'you aim to come along with me?"

"What way are you travelin'?" asked Slim.

"West to——"

"I'm beatin' south to Barneytown. So long—and thanks for all the news!"

You will have a somewhat clearer understanding of this son of the wilderness when I tell you that even after what he had heard from the cowpuncher, he was not half sure that Stan Geary was really dead. The dread of that monster with his long, thick, gorilla arms, and his vast, monkey face, remained constantly in the heart of Slim; and as he made his preparations for departure, he had a sense of guilt and fear; and constantly he was looking toward the southern hills, as though he half expected the familiar, bulky outline of Geary to loom above the horizon. What he intended, first of all, was to go to Barneytown and make sure of the great tidings which he had just heard. If he could see the grave with the name of Geary on the tombstone, then he would be moderately certain that his persecutor was indeed no more. What he would do after that, he hardly knew; the time would tell him as the occasion arose.

But it did not come into his mind that he possessed information vital to Lew Melody; Slim could prove that Geary had been hired to go to Barney Valley for the express purpose of murdering Melody, and that evidence would most certainly take the imputation of a murder from the shoulders of the fugitive.

So the desert rat trekked south. Sometimes he jogged the mustang remorselessly along; sometimes in rough country he dropped from the saddle and ran ahead, with the little horse following like a dog at his heels; it saved the strength of the animal, and it gave Slim a chance to express in physical action some of his burning desire to go to Barneytown. It was a march made almost at railroad speed; and when Slim came into Barneytown, he wasted no time, but made instant inquiries after the fate of the giant.

TWELVE

Mrs. Cheswick arrived at our house after her choir practice. She was full of news, full of excitement, full of tears. Of course I asked first of all if Sandy Furnival had come in for the rehearsal, and I was a happy man to hear Mrs. Cheswick say that she had. This was the first time since the day when she had broken with Lew Melody.

"And how does she look?" said I. "And what does she say? And did she seem happy to be singing again?"

Mrs. Cheswick shook her head in answer to everything. The good woman really had tears in her eyes, while she told us that Sandy was a ghost of her old self, with her face wan and her eyes spiritless.

"But it was old Mrs. Kingdon who made her lose her self-control though. She came running in to ask if we had heard the news. We asked her what she meant, and—of course the half-blind old thing didn't see Sandy. She blurted out the cream of the news in one breath. It was too much for Sandy. When she heard that the posse was getting ready to ride, and that Bill Granger and Doc Newton were going with it after him, she staggered up from her chair with a choked sort of a cry and left the church. I tried to stop her. I couldn't. She gave me one desperate look, and I couldn't say a word to her."

"But what news was it?" cried Mrs. Travis and I in one breath.

"What news? Why, it's been in town for more than half an hour! The posse is gathering as fast as it can. Deputy Sheriff Sid Marston had sent all over Barneytown for the best fighting men that he can get; and they're riding out at once."

"For what, Mrs. Cheswick? For what, in heaven's name?"

"Is it possible that you haven't heard!" cried she. "But Lew Melody has robbed the bank at Comanche Crossing!"

Just what story Mrs. Cheswick told us of that wild adventure, I forget. What I know now is the full story as I gathered it from a dozen different sources later on.

When Melody left the sheriff lying by the watering trough with a bullet hole through his right shoulder, he had ridden back that night to say a last good-night to Sandy Furnival and try—vainly—to make her change her mind. Then he had turned north and held steadily to the rough upper hill country, probably killing his food as he went; for he was glimpsed only twice, and both times by hunters for game, not for man! Both reports represented him going steadily north and north.

But he had apparently wearied of this dull life, with nothing but the mountains to keep him company, and so he turned straight back and came out of the hills and down into the upper part of Barney Valley until he reached the old Indian ford where the rich little town of Comanche Crossing had grown up. It was not more than fifty miles from Barneytown itself, and I suppose that there must have been half a hundred men in Comanche Crossing—to put it mildly—who had seen Lew Melody face to face. Besides that, the description of him was everywhere, together with posters which showed an excellent likeness of him, taken the year before when he had won the bucking contest at the rodeo at Twin Rivers. In spite of all this, Lew Melody had dared to ride into Comanche Crossing in the middle of the day and straight down the street on the bay horse which he had taken from Sheriff Joe Crockett.

He had gone to the bank and dismounted and thrown the reins of his horse just in front of the main door of the little building from which half of the mining and the ranching of the valley was financed. Then he had sauntered in and gone to a bench at the side of the room. There he sat down and lighted a cigarette which the doorkeeper-janitor came to him and told him he would have to put out, because there was a bank regulation against smoking in the building—which was of wood.

Lew Melody had answered so pleasantly, and put out the cigarette so obediently, that the janitor had fallen into conversation with him about the major topic of the day, so far as our mountains were concerned, and that was about Lew Melody himself! The janitor had a theory that Lew was striking toward Canada.

While they were chatting, the line in front of the cashier's window melted away, and when there was no one there, Lew Melody excused himself from the janitor and walked up to the window and asked for a blank check and a pen.

The cashier gave it to him and he wrote across the check: "Please pay me ten thousand dollars in large bills and about five hundred in small ones. Lewis Melody."

This little note he shoved under the window to the cashier and then dropped a significant right hand upon his hip and waited.

The cashier read that note and looked up with a grin; but the grin went out when he studied the grave eyes of Lew. He remembered the pictures which he had seen; and suddenly the surety came to him that this was the man—and not a joke at all!

I know that people have been fond of criticizing that poor cashier for cowardice. He had a revolver lying on the bench just beneath his window. All he had to do was snatch it up and fire it into the breast of Lew Melody.

That is to say, unless Lew Melody was able to get his own weapon out first and plant his shot in time. And, considering that Lew's weapon was in its holster, that likelihood seemed very far distant! However, can one really blame the clerk? I put myself in his place, and honestly say that I cannot. If those steady gray eyes looked into mine and made such a demand upon me—why, I am sure that I would have done exactly what the cashier did—that is to say, I should have gone to the open safe and taken out a sufficient quantity of money and carried it back to the window. And there I should have passed it over to Lew Melody.

This, at least, is what the poor man did, and Melody backed toward the front door, chatting still with the janitor in a lively manner, but keeping his deadly eye fixed upon the cashier. So he reached the door and leaped out of it, just as the cashier yelled the bad news to the rest of the employees.

Of course they snatched up weapons and poured out onto the street, but all they saw of Lew was the flash of the tail of the bay horse as he jerked that animal around the next corner and fled for the hills again.

Meanwhile at the jail, Deputy Sid Marston, who was taking the place of Joe Crockett while the sheriff was recovering from his wound, was gathering a select group of riders and fighters.

He was about ready to make his start. He had with him only seven men and seven horses, but every man was an ideal frontiersman and every horse was an ironlimbed devourer of mileage. Sid Marston called them around him and made a speech.

He said: "Boys, we're not starting out to make a little dash up country, beat around a while, lose the trail, and come back with tired hosses and a pile of wasted time behind us. We've got to match up agin' a shifty lad who knows those mountains and the desert as well as any of us. He's got a hundred thousand square miles of hole-in-the-wall country to run around in; and we're gunna be beating around pretty much in the dark, most of the time. But he's got to be landed, and it's worth while landing him.

"He's got to be landed because he's gone all wrong. Ever since he was fourteen he's been raising hell, but the hell he raised was mostly over in the Mexican section of Barneytown with thugs from both sides of the border. Well, boys, that was all right. It wasn't the sort of fun that you and me would want to fool around with. But it didn't bother us none while he was usin' up bullets on thugs. But now he's changed. He's got the blood taste. About the killing of Geary—well, I dunno that that was so bad. Geary had a record of his own. But anyway, that's a murder charge. And then comes the shooting of Joe Crockett. Well, that's different. And after that, he swiped Crockett's hoss. Boys, a hoss thief is a skunk, as you all know. A hoss is a thing that a gent's life is apt to depend on. In this here country where it might be sixty miles to a water hole, the gent that swipes a hoss don't deserve no more kindness than we'd show to a rattlesnake. But that ain't enough for Lew Melody: things get dull for him. So he slides down out of the hills and takes ten thousand dollars out of a bank. I ain't saying nothing about the men up there in Comanche Crossing. I think, though, that he couldn't of got away with that in Barneytown.

"We got a duty to get this Lew Melody, because we're sort of responsible for the things that he's done. On the other hand, it wouldn't be such a bad job to finish off. The bank is offering two thousand reward, besides a percentage of any of the bank's money that we should get back on him. And they's close to fifteen hundred put up by other gents in the valley. Before we nail him, you can lay to it that the reward will be around four or five thousand dollars, and if you split that into eight chunks, it leaves a pretty good salary for each one of us. That's the money side of it.

"All right, I say that if we start out and plan to stick to this job, and not put in three days, but six weeks at it, we got a chance to land our friend Lew Melody. Them that don't want to make a good, long campaign of it, can step out now. The rest of us will go on."

No one fell out of the party on account of these remarks. It merely made them look upon the work before them more soberly; but Sid Marston had chosen these fellows with care and had known beforehand, quite accurately, what they would think and what they would do. He had finished his little address and they had signified their acceptance on the conditions with a murmur and then silence, when Marston added: "We'll travel light, with small packs. But if any of you hasn't along as much as he thinks he'll need for a six-week roughing trip through the mountains, go home and get the odds and ends."

There was no answer to this; each was prepared to start as he stood.

The little crowd which had gathered to see the posse start fell back to give them room to ride away when a voice said: "It ain't all right, Marston. You got eight men, and that ain't lucky."

Sid Marston, very well satisfied with everything that had gone before, looked with a grin upon the lithe form of Slim as that ragged youngster pushed his mustang forward.

"What might be a lucky number, son?" said he.

"Nine!" said Slim.

"Might you be the ninth man for us?" asked the deputy, beginning to guess what was coming.

"I'm the man you want," said Slim with much assurance.

For the news which he had heard about hundreds of dollars in reward for the capture of the criminal had filled his imagination completely. And from the grim, efficient look of this troop of fighters, he felt sure that even the giant who had destroyed Stan Geary must fall before them.

His suggestion was received with a chuckle from the posse and a roar of laughter from the bystanders.

"You got a hoss," said the deputy mildly, "that ain't got the looks of a speedster."

There was another laugh at that.

"Old Sam," said the boy, "will start you all laughin' on the other side of your face. He'll stay with you. He ain't got the looks, but he's got the stuff in him! Besides, I don't weigh as much as the rest of you."

"Suppose that you was to stay on the trail," said the deputy, "are you pretty much of a fightin' man, kid?"

"I'll show you," said the boy.

He raised the old rifle and looked around him for a target, while the crowd nudged one another and chuckled expectantly. But what the boy chose was the staff of a weather vane which stood above the new jail.

"That rooster up there," said Slim, "looks pretty sassy, so—"

And he tucked the butt of the rifle into the hollow of his shoulder, steadied the heavy barrel with his sinewy hands, and drew his bead on the line of moonlight which ran along the gilded staff of the weathercock. Then he fired.

But the rooster remained undaunted in his post. There was a loud yell of derision and amusement from the crowd, and Marston began: "The cocksure man or the cocksure kid ain't always—"

He stopped abruptly, for there was a shout of astonishment from all those people as they saw the weathercock sway and then sag forward and drop from his staff. The bullet from the boy's rifle had cut through the staff, but still the vane was supported by a few shreds of wood and the pressure of the first puff of wind was needed to tumble the cock down.

"There you are," said Slim, highly gratified by the surprise and the applause. "And that ain't all that I can do. I'll hit a mark no bigger'n that rooster with a knife, and I'll live on half what you big gents need. Does that sound good to you, Mr. Deputy Sheriff?"

Marston scratched his head. Of course he felt that he could not take this confident little imp along, but he also felt that it would be unfair to refuse him a place point-blank after he had passed such an entrance test.

"We're beating north," said he. "If you're with us when sunup comes, you can stay along with us as long as your hoss lasts for the work. That's all I can do for you!"

Slim regarded the other horses with a solemn eye and then nodded. "That's easy!" said he, and when the eight men with Marston in the lead jogged with a jingling of bits and spurs and a creaking of saddle leather down the street, Slim brought up the rear on his nondescript pony.

THIRTEEN

When it was found that Slim was still in the rear of the party and his ugly mustang traveling along without signs of very great effort, Marston passed the covert word among his men to increase the pace to a marked degree and let their horses out. He set the example, and for the next ten miles those fine animals worked hard up the valley. But at the end of ten miles, as Marston slackened the gait a little, the shadowy form of Slim came bobbing up from the rear!

The problem of the boy became a more and more serious one. And so, at length, Marston decided to have his party ride their horses out that night. A thorough rest would let them recuperate the next morning; besides, it would perhaps be as well to cover the first stages of the journey with a rush and get into the upper mountains toward which the bank robber had fled. And, in addition to all this, his primary object was to shake off that tenacious youngster. So he freshened the pace of the party again and through the night he drove them remorselessly onward to the dawn. But when the pink of the morning came, and the deputy turned in his saddle to look back over Barney Valley, far beneath him, with the river curving in a pink ribbon through the midst, the first thing that he saw, over the top of the next hill below him, was the form of a slender boy running strongly up the steep slope, with a mustang jogging at his heels.

At that, Sid Marston understood how the ugly little pony had been able to keep up with the party, and his heart jumped a little in admiration of this persistent youngster. He was grave the next moment. It went against the grain to deny the boy after Slim had put forth such an effort and worked all night, but, obviously, the posse could not go into action with any such child in the ranks. If a bullet from the sure rifle of Lew Melody should strike down this boy, it would be a blot upon the repute of Marston that could never be rubbed out.

First he invited Slim to breakfast with them. On the shoulder of a hill, in a thick cluster of pines, the tired men made their bivouac and there Slim ate bread and bacon and drank black coffee with the rest; then they rolled themselves in their blankets.

It was late in the morning when they were wakened by the signal of Marston, telling them: "The hosses are rested, even if we ain't; and we sleep no more than the hosses do on this here trip. Turn out, boys!"

They rose, stifling their groans, for the ride of the night before had taxed the strength of the best of them. While they made ready to depart, Sid Marston called Slim to him and they sat down on the edge of a boulder which looked down on the dipping hills to the valley, a dizzy distance beneath them, with the Barney River, like silver, in the midst. "Slim," said the deputy sheriff, "I've got to tell you something that takes the heart out of me. I've got to tell you that this here job that we got on our hands is all for men, and not for boys!"

He expected an outburst of rage and perhaps tears at the end. But Slim, sitting slouched forward and with his chin in his brown palm, merely turned his head slowly to the side and regarded the deputy with a look of scorn and weariness in his dusty-black eyes.

"I knowed that something like that was coming," said Slim.

The deputy bit his lip. "After you showed so much nerve in you, I didn't have the heart to turn you down flat. But when I looked at the stumpy legs of that mustang of yours, I figgered that you wouldn't have a chance to keep up with the party. And that's why I told you that if you were with us in the morning, I'd let you keep along with the party. Y'understand?"

"Aw, the devil," said Slim, "I understand, right enough!"

"Now, I ain't gonna send you back with nothing for your work. Here's twenty dollars, kid. You take that. It ain't bad for a day's work, like you've had."

Slim regarded the bill blankly. It was more money than he had seen in his life before, with a chance to call it his own, but now it meant nothing to him. All night he had lain awake by fits and starts, or fallen asleep to dream of himself standing among the dead of the posse, leveling his rifle and firing the shot which brought the dreadful Lew Melody to his death. And after that—he had seen himself acclaimed as a hero by the thousands.

He had looked at his picture in newspapers. And he had spent a long time translating six hundred dollars into other terms. There was almost nothing which six hundred dollars would not do. It would clothe one from head to foot. It would give him underwear, to begin with—Slim had almost forgotten what that term meant. It would gird him with a cartridge belt supporting the finest of revolvers. It would seat him on a glorious horse—one that floated over the ground, rather than pounded along upon it, as poor Sam did! And it would put upon his head a sombrero enriched with Mexican gold and silver work; and it would mount him on a rich saddle, glittering with metal, and in the long holster beneath his knee would be the shining length of the finest repeating rifle. And in the pack behind his saddle he would have a little hand ax of the truest steel; the knife in his belt would be a razor-edged minister of death; he would have a true wool blanket; his boots would be shop-made of bright leather.

And when all this was accomplished, would there not still be very much of the six hundred left? Slim felt that there would—certainly enough to last him until he came on the trail of another man that needed catching. And with such a rifle, and such a revolver and knife, and with such a horse beneath him, what human being could escape from him?

So he dropped his glance from his glorious vision to a wretched twenty-dollar bill.

"What's this for?" he said.

"For you and your work and the nerve you have, son!" said the deputy kindly.

"I don't want it," said Slim.

"It's yours," said Marston, and putting it down on the rock beside Slim, he stood up.

"Wait a minute," said Slim. "Are you pretty sure that you don't want this no more?"

"It ain't mine," said Marston.

"Then I can do what I want with it?"

"Sure," said Marston. "A kid like you ought to find plenty of spending in twenty dollars, I guess!"

"Aw, well," said Slim, "I s'pose that you figger it that way. This is the way I spend chicken feed like that!"

He wrapped the bill around a rock and flung it far and true down the slope until stone and money splashed in the foaming waters of a little creek.

Then the boy cried: "Stay with you? Why should I want to stay with you? You and your bunch of bums, they couldn't catch rabbits if they were all greyhounds, which they ain't. Stay with you, naw—I'm sick of you!"

The deputy, biting his lip with anger, endured all of this reproof, because he felt that he had earned it; he held his tongue and watched Slim stalk in dignity to the despised mustang, Sam, and then ride slowly down the slope toward the hollow where the gray roof of a house appeared among the trees. Marston, taking note, bit his lip and groaned again, for he saw that the boy was not taking the back trail to Barneytown.

But once Slim was out of sight of the deputy and the rest of the men, he flung himself onto the ground and burst into a wildcat fury, tearing at his hair, beating the ground with naked heels and brown fists, spitting and cursing and moaning in a frenzy of rage. He even started at a run, stealthily, up through the trees, swinging his rifle at the trail beside him. But as he ran, he heard the noise of hoofs start off down the slope of the mountain, heading still north and west.

Then Slim paused and leaned his hand against a tree, a boy very sick at heart and very weak of spirit, hanging his head, and wishing heartily that he had never been born into such a world of liars, sneaks, and scoundrels. Compared with such conduct as this, even Stan Geary had qualities worthy of some admiration!

So thought Slim, and sat down for a moment with his head in his hands.

But who could sink down the trail and surrender to gloom when there had been such golden visions to cheer him only the night before? He started up again and ran back toward poor Sam. For he told himself, that if the deputy and his clan had a chance to capture Lew Melody, so did he! And four thousand dollars—

He waved his hands above his head and laughed with joy. Now he could bless the fate which he had been cursing the moment before. Four thousand dollars—for himself—riches—riches beyond calculation! For, if he attempted to list the very articles on which such a vast sum could be spent, how could he do it? He tried, and his brain failed him. If a stout pocketknife cost thirty-seven cents, how many pocketknives could be purchased for four thousand dollars?

Confusion, but the confusion of a heavenly bliss!

He, too, rode north and west.

FOURTEEN

The next bulletin which we had concerning the activities of Lew Melody was brought to us by a special messenger from the fighting front. He came down the valley riding on the bay horse of Sheriff Joe Crockett, which Lew had in the first place stolen. And he brought with him a letter to the sheriff. It read:

Dear Sheriff Crockett: The bearer is being paid for riding the way back to you. I apologize for running away with the horse, but the boys seemed pretty much set to blow me to bits when they came at me out of the bunkhouse.

So I thought that my own pony, which was pretty fagged, wouldn't have a chance to make a fast getaway. I borrowed the bay, and here it is back again. He may be a little thin, but I haven't had to press him hard at any time. He's a wonder; and if I last long enough at this new job of mine, maybe you'll catch me on him!

If that luck comes to anybody, I hope that it comes to you! Because of all the square sheriffs that ever threw a leg over a saddle, you're squarest and the whitest. And if I had the thing to do over again, I'd stand still and let you put the irons on me. But I couldn't, that day. I thought of jail, and being tried for murder—that's a black word! And if I got away from hanging, I thought that it would mean a good many years in the penitentiary, and so here I am, up to my neck in it.

Not that I really repent. No, you can tell the boys that I'm having the time of my life.

I've had to have another horse; and

the one I've taken is the Gray Pacer. I suppose you know all about it!

Best luck to you on all trails—even on mine!

Lew Melody.

This odd letter was received with a transport of enthusiasm by the entire population of Barneytown. There was something jovially daredevil and carefree about it that appealed to all Western hearts. And, besides this appeal, that letter was brought by a man who carried back the bay horse to the sheriff. And then, to turn the matter into a greater jest than ever—while returning one horse and liberally paying a man to make the trip back with it, he had stolen another and far more valuable one!

I hastened to Joe Crockett to get his reactions to that letter, and I found that honest man thoroughly stricken.

"All I wish is this," said Crockett: "That Stan Geary had dropped into the middle of the earth before he ever come to Barney Valley to raise hell here."

"Aside from the swearing," said I, for it always annoyed me to have the sheriff speak as though my profession were as vulgar a one as his own, "aside from the swearing, I'm tempted to agree with you; but the more I think of the thing, the more I see that it had to come about. In one way or another, Lew Melody was sure to break the law before the end. He had too much strength and he plunged too much to be kept in any harness ever made by the law."

"D'you think so?" said the sheriff. "Well, I dunno. But now the good he's done is forgot, and nothing but the last things he's done is remembered!"

When I reached Barneytown again, I heard the complete story of the stealing of the Gray Pacer, which I had overlooked in the excitement. It had seemed no more than a small incident, compared with the return of the bay horse to Crockett and the letter to the sheriff which accompanied the return of the animal. But now I learned that it was something more—a great deal more!

I had heard of the Gray Pacer, of course. I suppose that every one in the entire country knew about it at the time of his capture; it made the sort of a story that newspapers like because of their color. The Gray Pacer was a mustang stallion—big, fierce, wise, and incredibly swift. Three years before he had made his appearance on the range—he was probably two or three at that time. Then his age at the moment of his capture was from five to six. He was no dwarfed thing, but a splendid creature of more than twelve hundred pounds, with all of that weight so beautifully distributed over his body that he did not appear to stand within a hundred and fifty pounds of his real weight.

His career was a costly one to the horse breeders in the mountain valleys. This cunning devil seemed to know by instinct exactly how to open corral gates, and once he had a gate open, he knew how to lure the mares out after him. Again and again he built up formidable bands of the finest horse stock on the range, and again and again the ranchers organized hunting parties which ran the bands down. They could recapture those of the mares which had not been killed by accident or ruined by overhard running. But they could not hurry the Gray Pacer. It was said that he had never broken his pace at any time. I suppose that one reason for this was that he kept very much to broken country, and up hill and down, a gallop is not so good as a smoother gait. But even across the

126

open country, his four legs of iron, stockinged with shining black silk, carried him away from all pursuit.

In the meantime, the damage he had done mounted into thousands and thousands of dollars, not only on account of horses which were swept off in his band and which were lost there, but also on account of the vast efforts which were made to capture the equine rascal. Bands of a dozen men and more laid elaborate traps for him, took out strings of their best horses, and worked a month at a time to get the fleet-footed beauty.

It began to seem probable that no one would ever be able to put a rope upon this shining flash of a horse, until Ches Logan, hunter extraordinary, appeared on the scene.

Ches was a man who did not know the points of a horse from the points of a cow. He had never used anything but mules and burros in his profession—which was trapping. But the skill of Logan was concentrated for the perfection of one art. He had arms of steel and an eye as sure as the eye of an eagle; with a rifle he was a master.

So, with a burro behind him to pack his

food, and with a rope coiled on top of the pack, and with his rifle slung across his back, and with a fat reward of more than a thousand dollars—I believe—hung up by the ranchers to encourage him, Ches Logan started forth to capture the Gray Pacer. Luck brought him within fair range of the big horse in ten days, and the rifle did the rest. A bullet, aimed with a skill beyond praise, nicked the spinal column of the stallion high up on the neck toward the head, where the cord is close to the surface of the flesh. The Gray Pacer dropped, and before its senses cleared, Ches Logan had secured it with hobbles.

He drove the horse out of Elkhorn to a little shack half a mile from the edge of the town. There he closed in a corral with a lofty board fence, and put the Gray Pacer inside. Thereafter, whoever chose could look as long as he pleased at the stallion, but for every visit the charge to pay was one dollar! It was said that a hundred came the first day, and thereafter, though the numbers diminished, Ches Logan ran a very profitable little show which beat trapping in ten ways. He had only to sit down and enjoy his pipe, look at the mountains, which tumble up to the sky around Elkhorn, and cook his meals. Money rolled into his hands without his labor.

Then, on a warm evening, a man stood in the open door of his shack, and he found himself looking into the face of none other than Lew Melody. There was no chance to reach his rifle; besides, at close quarters, what chance had a rifle against the revolver which was sure to come like lightning into the hand of Melody. The trapper merely nodded and said: "Come in, Lew, and rest your feet. How's things?"

So Lew came in and sat down. He wasted no time.

"I want the Gray Pacer," said he. "What's the price?"

Ches Logan looked at the holstered gun of Melody and answered: "I suppose the price of one slug is about all you'll have to pay for him."

"You have the wrong idea," answered Melody. "I've come to buy that horse."

"Money," said Logan, "is all I'm making out of him."

"You've taken the cream already," said Melody. "You're not making very much now. There were only five people here today, and before the winter comes, that'll dwindle to two or three."

"Two or three dollars is wages for me," said Logan. "I ain't one of these here proud gents. I live pretty simple."

"There's a price on everything," said Melody. "I'm not offering a hundred or two hundred. I'll give you five hundred dollars in cash."

"Look here," said Logan. "If you want that hoss, why don't you take it?"

"I don't rob poor men," said Melody.

"If I was to take your money, wouldn't the bank at Comanche Crossing take it back again?" asked Logan.

"That money I got from them wasn't marked," said Lew. "They could never touch it. Besides," went on Melody, "there was never a saddle on that stallion. I have to break him in. And every time I have to make a trip down to him, at night, you'll collect a hundred dollars."

"Is that a go?" said Logan. "D'you think that you can break him in five tries?"

"I think so."

"Well, son, you shake on that with me!" said Logan. "You pay me a hundred dollars a trip and I'll sell the hoss to you as soon as he's broke."

"You think he's unbreakable?" asked Melody.

"I don't think; I know," said Logan. "He ain't a hoss; he's a tiger."

"Well," said Melody, "I'm ready to start the payments before I've seen him. Here's a hundred now!"

So Logan took that money and they went out where Melody could get at the Gray Pacer and Logan could sit by to smoke his pipe and watch. What they both saw was worth seeing. Melody found a wild devil disguised as a horse, and maddened by the blind confinement behind those tall walls of the fence. It is not hard to imagine what the Gray Pacer was at that time. I have seen six-hundred-pound mustangs with more life than a wildcat and more venom than a rattlesnake. But those were ratty little geldings; even so, it took a mighty skillful rider to keep in the saddle for half a minute. But here was twelve hundred pounds of shapely stallion, with the freedom and the kingship of the open range behind him and a thorough conviction that his one grand purpose in life was to set his teeth in the first man that he could reach, or drive his heels through the body of a victim.

But Lew Melody started his work, and he did it without haste. He was paying a hundred dollars for every try, and that rate was enough to make most men anxious. However, the nerves of Melody were adjusted perfectly for just such trials. He went calmly to work and acted as though time was nothing in his estimation. That first night he tamed the stallion only sufficiently to take an apple from his hand— and try to eat the hand as well as the apple! But Melody was not discouraged.

He came down a second time and paid another hundred dollars, and on that night he appeared to have lost ground. The third night he made greater progress. The fourth night, the stallion was wilder than at first, and Melody, looking along the glimmering flanks of the beautiful beast in the starlight, saw a shadow which looked like the long welt of a whip.

He said to Logan: "You've been out here tormenting this stallion. Logan, tonight's money goes for tomorrow night besides!"

That was the beginning of hard feeling between them; but Logan saw that it would be dangerous to try to trick the outlaw any more. He sat still and contin-

ued to collect his hundred dollars for each
visit from Lew Melody.

FIFTEEN

I have often thought of the oddity of that
bargain between the trapper and the
outlaw. Both were as nearly lawless as
could be imagined, and yet I suppose that
the nearest approach to a law-loving spirit
was in Melody and not in Logan. If Ches
had not broken the law, it was merely
because a trapper does not often have a
chance to invade the rights of other men.

But, in the meantime, it was a delightful
experience for him. He had proved that
his judgment was right in one respect, at
least. Five visits, even throughout the third
one, had not tamed the wild spirit of the
Gray Pacer, although each visit from Melody lasted from dark until dawn, when
he withdrew toward the rough mountains.
For he had come to this region not primarily because it was the place where he
could get the Gray Pacer, but because it
was an ideal hole-in-the-wall country. The
mountains swelled all around the valley in
which the little town of Elkhorn lay. They

were difficult, but not impassable, those mountain trails. A man who had a close knowledge of those trails had an immense advantage over those who did not know. And it was said that Melody, befriending a widow living in the hills, learned from her son as much about those trails as the mountain goats themselves could have told him.

It was a very broken country, indeed. There was not only the jumble of the rocks and the steep cliffs, but there was the manifold problem presented by many little streams which raced down from the snows and choked the Elkhorn River with their burdens of mud and of pebbles and rolled stones. Some of those arrowy little currents could be leaped by a fine horse; but no horse in the world could wade through the raging currents. And again, there were places where the waters pooled a little, running over flats, and these could be swum or forded. But these places were continually changing as the furious waters hewed new destinies for themselves through soil or hard rock. To combine with all of this, was the heavy foresting of mighty trees in the lower valleys shading to marching ranks of lodge-pole pines which walked away over the crests—except for those summits which lifted above timber line and carried their naked heads into the white region of snows. A stranger would never have found ground, except by accident, on which a horse could raise a gallop. But one familiar with the district could dip into good ground for a comfortable percentage of the traveling. And all the back country around Elkhorn was of a similar nature. It was no wonder that other criminals before Lew Melody had fled to this district; it was no wonder that Lew himself had found it.

But what he primarily needed, in such a region, was a horse with the endurance of a mule and the sure footing of a mountain goat. Otherwise it was really better to travel on foot. As for the big, lumbering bay of the sheriff, so excellent to stretch away across level going, it was of very little use here. One must have an animal which moved upon springs, and which had been educated to mountain work—one which could tell what slope must be coasted down on braced legs, because the soil was loose, and what slope could bear the weight of driving hoofs and a heavy body. He needed a horse which could leap the narrow streams without being frightened by their great voices, which could walk along a rock ledge a foot wide without growing dizzy at the thousand feet of nothingness which dropped on one side or the other; a horse with limbs of steel and a heart of steel also. And here was wild Gray Pacer made to his hand! No wonder he was willing to risk his life itself in order to gain such a mount. It was as though he were adding wings to himself and leaving earth dwellers, to find safety among the birds.

The excellent Ches Logan appreciated this very well. And sometimes he cursed himself because he had not set the price at two hundred dollars a visit instead of one hundred. However, the bargain had been made, and he saw that he would have to stick to it unless he wished to have a bullet from an unerring Colt crash among his ribs, or unless he could devise some cunning expedient.

The expedient at last came to him. It was not an honorable one, but what Ches Logan wanted, after a life of hard labor, was plenty of money and plenty of ease. What he decided to do, finally, was to betray Lew Melody to the men of the law who resided in the town of Elkhorn. He made a trip to the town, therefore, and in very vague and general terms suggested that, with good luck he hoped one day to be able to lead them to Lew Melody. He wanted to know what his share of the reward would be, if he took no actual hand in the danger of the capture. And the answer was that one half would come to him.

It was enough. The thought of two thousand dollars in addition to the thousand he had made from the capture of Gray Pacer, the extra hundreds which had been poured into his coffer by the show which he had conducted, and the additional money which he had received from the hand of Lew Melody himself—these items all united to form a fund which was well above contempt. With some little management and moderation in his scheme of living, he could exist for the rest of his days upon that sum. And Ches Logan decided that the time had come for him to seize opportunity by the forelock and retire while the way was opened before him.

He made his visit to the town after the fifth night trip of Melody to the shack, but still he could not make up his mind to betray Melody at once. Every additional trip which the outlaw made added another hundred dollars to the coffers of wise Ches Logan. And a hundred dollars is the price of how many coyote furs, gained by how many miles of hard trudging, and how many hours of dirty, disagreeable work?

The sixth visit from Melody saw him bring down his saddle and actually succeed in fastening it upon the back of Gray Pacer. But still he had not sat in the saddle as yet, and the trapper scratched his chin and bided his time. The seventh visit, however, saw Melody sitting in that saddle; and though it was with an uneasy seat, and though Gray Pacer was as uneasy as a wild colt under this strange burden, yet he did actually answer the reins a little. And Logan saw that the time had come.

Dawn was not bright on the next day, and Melody was not gone an hour, when Logan started from his shack and walked hastily into the town. There he told his story. Which was, simply, that Lew Melody, tired of his lonely life in the mountains, had formed the habit of slipping down from the mountains and chatting for an hour or so in the evening at the house of the trapper.

The very next evening he had promised to pay his host a visit, and therefore Ches Logan invited the officers of the law to come to his shack and secrete themselves there. Who could have resisted such an invitation? No matter how much they despised the treachery of Ches Logan, all men know that it takes a rascal to catch a rascal.

They made their plans with care, and they gathered eight good men and true to march out to the shack. Four were to hide in the brush outside the cabin. Four more were to wait quietly indoors, to provide an unexpected reception committee for the desperado. With this plan arranged, they started out from the town at noon and walked to the shack.

But when they came in view of the little house, they were surprised to find a tall bay horse tethered outside the door to a sapling at which it was contentedly chewing, raking off the tender bark.

"It looks," said some one, "a devilish lot like the hoss of that Sheriff Joe Crockett, away down in Barneytown!"

So they scattered like Indians in a circle around the shack. It seemed incredible that Lew Melody should have risked a daylight visit to the shack, but there stood the bay horse, answering point for point the description with which they were all so familiar, and of which many of them had dreamed by night.

They stole up on the shack on their hands and knees, taking advantage of every bit of covert. When they were close, they charged the front door with a yell, struck it, burst it from its hinges, and rushed in upon an empty room!

No, not quite empty. There was no Lew Melody there, but upon the little deal table in the center of the apartment were two hundred-dollar bills, nailed down into the wood. There was a message beneath each one, and on top of one there was secured a letter addressed to Joe Crockett.

Beneath the first bill was this penciled message: "This money is for the man who will take this letter and ride the bay horse back to Barneytown and give both the horse and the letter to Sheriff Joe Crockett."

Beneath the second bill was a note for the eyes of Ches Logan, and it ran as follows:

Dear Ches Logan: You've been figuring

me away in the mountains, but, as a matter of fact, I've made my camp in those pines on the hill not five hundred feet from your shack. I saw you start for town, and if that trip means any good for me, I admit that I'm a fool.

But, in case my guess is wrong, I leave the last payment for the Gray Pacer. He's taken to me at night. I would have worked a couple of more nights with him, but I suppose that I'd better risk a trip on him now rather than wait to see what you might bring back with you from Elkhorn.

If I'm wrong about you, I give you my apologies now.

If I'm right about you, and you really meant to double cross me, then all I have to say is that Elkhorn and every other place in the mountains is bad medicine for you. Take my advice and go East—far East! They have healthier air out that way!

Lew Melody.

The first rush was to the inclosure where the Gray Pacer had been kept. But the corral was empty! And when they searched the ground near by, they saw not far away a patch of soft earth which told of a deadly struggle between the half-tamed horse and the half-wild master. The ground had been torn up by plunging heel, and here and there were broad marks where the big animal had flung itself down in an effort to escape from the clinging rider. However, in the end the man must have won; for suddenly the trail stretched away in long gaps, showing how Gray Pacer had bolted off toward the mountains.

But the cruel part of it all, from my viewpoint, was that though Lew had paid for Gray Pacer, it needed only a flat denial from the trapper to put Melody down as a horse thief once more.

SIXTEEN

When the news came of the stealing of Gray Pacer, and the second escape of Lew, Cordoba was blank and silent.

"They will never be able to get him!" cried Juanita.

"Ah, girl," said her father. "Can you say that? Such things as he has done are always punished in the end!"

"How punished?" said Juanita, trembling. "And what has he done that is so bad? Was not Señor Geary a famous devil? Did he not deserve to die?"

"The law is the law," said Cordoba sadly. "Sometimes it is gentle as a lamb, and sometimes it is a hungry bear that tears out the hearts of men without any pity. So it will be with Don Luis, poor boy!"

This speech left a grave silence in the room, the señora looking anxiously at her daughter, and Juanita looking in blank terror straight before her.

Cordoba took out a pendant of three emeralds, held by a chain of gold.

"And yet," said he, "this little thing— this little bit of bright glass, you might say—could save his life and give him back to us!"

"Ah?" cried Juanita. "Can you mean that?"

"Do you not see, child? The price of this is far more than the ten thousand dollars which he stole."

"But horse thefts—and murder—"

"Well, I have enough money to stop the mouths of the ones who might talk of horse stealing. And as for the murder of that Señor Geary, I think that even if Don

Luis came to trial for it at this minute, when the minds of all men are so hot with him, he would be acquitted. He would be saved by such lawyers as I should hire for him. Ah, we would fight for him, would we not?"

Juanita ran to him and slipped onto his lap. She was trembling with joy.

If he loved her, he would give that little trio of stones to poor Don Luis. What was such a sum to her father, and was it not life to Don Luis? Besides, she, Juanita, would love her father twice as hard all her life if he did this one little good thing.

"So?" said Cordoba, smiling sadly at her. "Do you wish it so much? But do you not see, child, that it cannot be taken to him? And even if it were brought to him, he would refuse it!"

"It *can* be taken to him," said Juanita. "Ah, it *can* be done!"

"Why, girl," said the moneylender, "are there not hundreds of brave, wise men, trying to come even close enough to him to send a bullet through his heart?"

This was too much for the poor girl. She ran to throw herself on a couch and there broke into a passion of tears.

"What have I done?" asked Cordoba, expanding his hands toward his wife.

The señora looked upon him with eyes of fire. "Nothing—nothing!" said she. "Speak to her one more thing like this, and all her troubles will end. You will kill her, and she will not be here to bother you any more!"

Cordoba cast a glance of anguish at his wife, and then he went to sit beside Juanita.

"Look, child," said he, fumbling with a desperate mind for something which would soothe her. "Here are these. They are for you, Juanita. They are yours, my dear girl. Take them and forgive your stupid father!"

The small, soft hand of Juanita closed over the three emeralds. The fine chain of gold which bore them coiled like a bright little yellow snake across the transparent olive skin of her wrist.

Presently her sobbing ceased, and she gathered the trinket to her heart.

"See!" whispered the moneylender, delighted, to his wife. "She is only a child, still! She has taken the toy—now she will forget!"

But the señora merely stared at him and

sighed in despair. "You are always so far from her!" said she. "Do you call her a child? She is old enough to be a mother even now!"

Now, when the next day dawned, it seemed that Juanita had recovered her spirits wonderfully. The color was returning to her cheek, and two or three times during the day her mother was transfixed by hearing the voice of the girl raised in a snatch of song.

It was noted, too, that Juanita went out to the stable behind the house and spent much time caressing the little pinto mare which Lew Melody had given to her because she taught him to dance. That beautiful little creature she had not been able to look upon since Melody disappeared. But now it seemed to fit into her mood at once.

She asked for money. What she asked for in that house was never questioned; she took what she would, but her mother had not more than a few dollars at the moment, and so she sent Juanita down to her father's counting room. There, sitting on his table and thereby throwing a pile of important papers into hopeless confusion, she teased his wallet from him and extracted from it a whole handful of bills.

"Merciful heaven!" cried Cordoba. "You have taken hundreds! I shall be a pauper."

And he laughed at her, delighted. There was no pleasure in his life so keen as the joy of filling her hands with whatever her heart desired.

She took this money on a strange shopping tour which carried her, first of all, to the big store, which was an emporium where everything the Mexican heart delighted in, from chilies to gold lace, could be bought. But her purchases made the storekeeper stare.

"It's a present," said Juanita. "Also, it is a secret!"

That evening Juanita could hardly be still for a moment. Dancing and singing and chattering, she filled their eyes with light.

"It is true," whispered the señora, "that she has dropped the thought of Don Luis from her heart!"

"Is she not my child? Do I not know her?" said the moneylender, more enchanted than ever. For he felt that he was about to conquer the admiration of his wife, even as he had won her love long before this day.

There was only one shadow on the evening, when Juanita ran to her father and took his burly head in her arms and whispered in his ear: "Whatever I do, will you always love me?"

"There is a question, foolish girl!"

"Tell me, though."

Afterward, to the señora, he said: "What could that mean?"

"Heaven only knows," answered his wife. "But there is something in her mind. It is not hard to guess that!"

What was in that mind they were far from dreaming. But when their voices had been stilled in their room for half an hour after dark, Juanita was up from her bed again. The bundle of her purchases was raised and opened—stealthily, stealthily. For how much noise, like a crashing of feet over dead leaves, the unfolding of stiff paper will make. And all must be done with the light of the lamp turned very low indeed!

She drew out from the package, finally, shining riding boots of the finest leather, and socks, and trousers, and a gay silk shirt, and a broad-brimmed sombrero, bright with metal work, and a broad belt of white goatskin with cartridge holders running around it, and a quirt, and a pair of golden spurs, and, strangest of all, a black leather holster with a neat .32 caliber revolver in it.

She took out this weapon and held it with both hands, and standing before the mirror, she leveled it at her image and made a face at the grim result. Then back went the revolver into the holster, and she was working at the clothes.

There were myriads of buttons, it seemed, to the unaccustomed fingers of Juanita, but when her slim body was clad in the new outfit, she ventured to turn up the flame of her lamp and view herself more fully. All was well, she thought, except for her head. And, even when she had crushed the sombrero well down, there was sure to be a curling lock in sight.

It needed a great heart, but she was determined. She tossed the sombrero on the bed, took out the pins, and allowed the shining weight of her hair to tumble to her waist. Then, with a scissors, she began to cut steadily. One glistening lock fell beside another on the floor as the steel cut through the masses. And, at last, the damage was done.

And what a change it was. Half the woman seemed to have been stolen from her face by that stroke. And when the hat was replaced, she felt a little tingling shock of surprise. For here was a boy, indeed, smiling back at her from the glass.

So, squinting sidewise judiciously at her image in the glass, she made a few strides up and down the room, as long as she could stretch them, and when she was ended, she decided that the impression was as masculine as anything she had ever seen.

Her confidence, which had been a badly shaken thing before, now seemed much restored. She gave one look and one sigh to the black and gleaming strands of hair upon the floor. So ended, she felt, her old life.

Then she scribbled on a piece of paper:

Dear Ones: I am going to take the emeralds to Don Luis. Forgive me and love me still if you can. I should have died if I had had to stay here, hearing every day of the troubles he lived in. Do not doubt that I shall find him and that I shall come back safely. You know that we have been in Elkhorn, and I remember the country around it very well.

Juanita.

So she gathered the last of her pack and rolled it in the slicker which she had not forgotten to buy with the rest. Then out with the light, while the blanketing darkness swept closely around her, a pause to make sure of her bearings—then through the door. Ah, how slowly, slowly she opened it. There seemed to be a coiled spring resisting her, but it was only the rust upon the hinges, and if she pressed too hard, a squeak began to develop. But the door was open at last.

Yet that was only the beginning of the dangers. Señor Cordoba could be depended upon to sleep heavily through all noises. Her mother, by the same token, could be depended upon to waken at the first stir, with all her faculties aroused. And here was a creaking floor to be crossed—how strange it was that she had never noticed the weakness of the floor before.

In spite of all her care and her time, there was a stealthy murmur from the floor

151

and, instantly a voice from the room of her mother: "Is it you, Juanita?"

"It is I, mother."

"Why are you up, child?"

"For a book."

"You must not stay awake to read. Go back to bed."

"Yes, mother!"

She rested a hand against the wall for a moment, to enable the blood to ebb out of her brain, for a dark mist of excitement was swirling there. Then she hurried down the stairs—but not too fast for fear—ah, there it was again—just before she reached the bottom of the flight, with the rear door of the house before her hand, a loud and heavy creaking sounded beneath the pressure of her foot.

And, from above: "Juanita!"

She did not answer. Desperate with haste, she opened the door and hurried out into the barnyard, and straight across it, running lightly on her toes, toward the stall of the pinto mare.

The devil possessed that fiery little creature. Fine feed and little exercise had made her like a frolicsome puppy. And it was a great task to settle the saddle on her back, and put the bit of the bridle between her teeth. And, when that was done, there was still the pack to be strapped on behind the saddle. But at this instant, she heard a loud scream from the house and she knew that the worst had come upon her. Her mother had grown suspicious, at last, and in the room of her daughter she had found the message of farewell.

After that, blinded with fear, she struggled with pack and straps, but, at last, the thing was somehow in place, while the windows were opening, and the voice of her mother was crying into the night: "Help! Help!" And yonder heavy thunder was the footfall of her father racing down the stairs of the house.

She was in the saddle and out of the barn in a flash and as the rear door of the house opened upon her father, lantern in hand, she swept past him, with the spurs glued to the sides of the pinto mare.

No main roads for Juanita. Instead, she swerved down dusty alleys and by-streets. When the pursuit started, it would rush north, according to the directions in her letter; but Juanita was riding south with might and main, and the little mare was flying with flattened ears and stretching neck through the night.

SEVENTEEN

It was not such a difficult trip. Not a sight or a sound of the pursuit that raged after her came to Juanita, but she drifted north and north, after her first southern detour, keeping always to the rough going of the mountain, and seeing hardly a living soul, except once a cow-puncher, who merely waved his hand from far off and jogged his horse on along the trail. But even that casual greeting gave heart to the girl, for she felt that it was an earnest of the success of her disguise.

And, as the sun browned her face and the backs of her hands more every day, she felt that she was fitting more accurately into her rôle. And so she came to the rugged mountain heads from which she could look down upon the rough valley in which lay Elkhorn—itself as rough as the mountains around it.

It was the midafternoon. And now that she was come upon the ground where her search must begin, what should she do first? She rode aimlessly until she came to the banks of a thundering stream; so great was the noise, and so heavily was it magnified in the damp, dark throat of the ravine, that Juanita expected to come out into view of the real river. But what she found was no more than a large brook, given such a roaring voice because of the arrowy steepness of the course it kept. It was impossible for the pinto to leap that stream; and when she urged the little beast down to attempt a fording, the pinto whirled with an angry snort and such sudden violence that the girl was nearly thrown.

She let the pinto wander up the bank of the stream for some distance, but it did not seem to diminish, and, as the evening was coming, she determined to pitch her camp in a pleasant clearing which she reached not far from the voice of the water.

There she built her fire, cooked her supper from the diminishing contents of her food pack, and rolled herself in her blanket. Pinto would be her guardian; and in an instant her eyes were closed.

It was, in fact, the snort of the mare that roused her, and made her sit up, blinking in the dying red of the firelight. She made out, before her, a shadowy form and the ray of light which traveled down the barrel of a rifle, leveled at her breast. The courage of Juanita ran like cold water out at her finger tips, and she threw her arms across her face.

"Aw, the devil," said a boy's voice. "It's nothin' but a kid!"

Juanita uncovered her face and found that the shadow in front of her, holding the rifle, was only a ragged imp—a veritable young wild man of the mountains with legs clad in bagging trousers which had been cut off, or frayed away to strings at the knees; while a very consummately dirty shirt covered the rest of the body of the boy. There was no covering upon his head except a dense thatch of sun-bleached hair. And the wild, bright eyes watched Juanita with the curiosity of an animal. Now the youngster lowered his rifle and leaned upon it. As he came closer to the light, she could see that there was a revolver strapped around his waist; and behind him loomed dimly the form of a ponylike horse with a ragged forelock hanging far down on its face.

She was reminded of a picture of some wild young Tartar about to leap on an enemy.

"What might you be doing up here?" asked the little savage.

"I'm looking for Lew Melody," said she.

"What?" barked out the other. "You lookin' for Lew Melody? And what would you do if you found him? Let him eat you?"

With this, his bare foot kicked onto the embers of the fire a dried branch of pine, full of resin, which flared up high at once and cast a wild yellow light over the clearing. By this light, which half blinded her, she saw the glittering eyes of the boy shining forth at her beneath a forelock as ragged as that of his horse.

"All right," said he, "you're gunna get this here Melody and bring him in by the nose, ain't you?"

"I didn't say that," said Juanita, repenting her frankness bitterly.

"Well," said the boy tyrannically, "I'm glad that you got *some* sense, because I'll tell you what you look like to me—you want to know?" He did not wait for her answer, but he continued with a savage heat: "You look like a softy to me! Y'understand?"

He came a fierce step nearer; and Juanita began to grow terrified in earnest. She

157

remembered her revolver in an unlucky moment and dropped her hand on the butt of it as she rose to her feet.

"Keep away from me," said she, with as much energy as she could summon. "Keep away from me, and don't—"

"Hey," yelled Slim, "you're just a sneaking coward! Are you?"

"I'm afraid that I am," said the girl.

At this hideous admission, Slim's strength gave way. He slumped down upon a fallen log and stared at her with his mouth agape.

"Oh, my Lord," breathed Slim. "I'd ruther of died than of said that to anybody. I'd of took more'n Stan Geary ever give me before I'd of said that! Tell me, what'll you ever do if you was to *see* this here Melody?"

"I don't know," said Juanita.

"Not me neither," said he with immense contempt. "I dunno what you'd do. But I tell you what—you'd better leave off wearin' guns, till you learn how to handle 'em. Why, if I'd had that gun and been where you was, and you where I was, why, I'd of blowed your belly clean out before you budged a step at me. But I could see by the way that you laid your

158

whole hand on that butt, instead of just the fingers, that you didn't know how to get it out fast. Otherwise I'd of finished you off quick and not waited to take it out of your hand. But it's a pretty slick gun, ain't it?"

"I don't know," shuddered Juanita. "You may have it, if you want it!"

The blood rushed to the face of Slim. He scooped up the revolver and examined it with a glistening eye.

"Would you be giving it to me?" he asked, in a hushed voice.

"Yes, yes," said the girl.

"Well," said Slim, burning with emotion, "I—I'd aim to pay you back for it—some day—when I got a chance—some day—"

"I don't want you to pay me back," said Juanita.

"The devil you don't!" breathed Slim, completely downed again with astonishment. For that so much cowardice and so much generosity could exist at the same moment and in the same breast, seemed to him an incredible thing. "Why," said Slim, "that's sort of generous—that's sort of—what made you give it to me?"

"Because you look as if you could use

it," said Juanita truthfully, and she added with a touch of flattery, as some of her courage began to return, "and because I hope that you'll be able to get me a sight of Lew Melody!"

For a burning instant he studied her, and then a broad grin began to form on his face; he stretched out a dirty hand.

"Shake!" said he. "You're lookin' on the gent that's gunna kill that big sucker Lew—and get the reward!"

"Kill him?" cried Juanita.

"Sure! Why not? I can shoot as straight as any man you ever seen. And I've worked out the thing that'll get him for me. I've worked it all out and done it this evening. Tomorrow I'm gunna get him sure!"

"How can you possibly do it!" asked the girl.

"I'll tell you, because I guess that you ain't gunna steal none of my fire. The other bums have been trying to find *him*, but I'm gunna make him try to find *me*. Y'understand? I'm gunna fetch him to me, and when we meet, let the best man win!"

The scheme of Slim was not without a considerable measure of ingenuity. According to his own code, a fairly rendered challenge was a thing which must perforce be recognized and accepted, and for that reason it was necessary that Lew Melody should meet in an equal fight with the readiness of any man of honor. Therefore he had worked out his plan.

He knew that, from the ready ease with which Melody had avoided many of the efforts to capture him, he must be receiving occasional word from friends of the movements which were being made against him. Accordingly, that evening the boy had gone to Elkhorn and on the bulletin board of the post office he had placed a large sheet of paper on which was scrawled the following message in large letters:

Lew Melody, listen to me:
Ime gunna ride down the Culver Cut tomorrer on a roan hoss. Ther ain't gonna be nobody but me along. Meet me ther and may the best man win.
Slim.

If this missive were misspelled, the spelling was not much worse than most of the mountaineers would have been capable of. And if the letters were formed with a shaking hand, they were at least large and

161

perfectly legible. Most of Elkhorn gathered to read this challenge and guess the reaction of Lew Melody when the news of it came to his ears; and great was the speculation as to the identity of Slim.

In the dawn, he was first awake, also.

"Hey, kid!" he sang out to her, and when she sat up, startled, he added: "You ain't told me your name?"

"Juan," said she. "And yours?"

"Me? I'm Slim. Folks'll know my name after today."

When breakfast was over, he donned his new clothes.

He had not had a chance to pick well in the obscure light of the store when he robbed it. His boots and his trousers were much too large. So was his coat. And yet, when he was equipped, and a felt hat slouched over his head, he did indeed look more like a man—all except the invincible youth of his face.

"But I got the way to fix that," declared Slim.

With his knife he combed out a bit of hemp rope of a fine weave, and finally produced two tufts which he affixed upon either side of his upper lip with daubs of glue. Juanita could not help smiling when

162

she was close, but, at a little distance, the effect was startlingly real. It added many a vital year to the boy's appearance.

So they started off for the Culver Cut. It was a strange experience for Juanita, but her reasoning was not without sense—it might indeed be that Lew Melody would answer the challenge which the boy had posted in the town. But when he arrived at the Cut, it seemed hardly probable to her that Melody could fail to see that Slim was none other than a young boy.

However, when, as Slim had instructed her, she followed him down the Cut at a safe distance in the rear, her heart began to misgive her. For, from the rear at least, he made a very convincing appearance of a mature man, and in the heat of a sudden meeting, with those ridiculous mustaches to help out the appearance, it was more than likely that if Lew Melody appeared suddenly out of the mouth of one of the many cross ravines which pierced the sides of the Cut, there probably would be a gun play before there had been a chance for any close examination of one another.

She had reached the decision and decided to hurry her mare ahead and try to dissuade the boy from his foolish attempt, when Slim with his roan mustang disappeared around the next curve of the Cut, and the next instant she heard a double report—the first a deep barking gun and the second the familiar, sharp, riflelike clang of the little .32 which Slim had been practicing with all the morning.

She gave the pinto the spurs then, and whirled around the next elbow of the valley wall in time to see Slim, poor man, stretched flat on his back while above him leaned the man she loved; and behind Lew Melody stood the most glorious horse that the girl had ever seen, a thing of silver, flaming beyond belief in the slant light of the morning.

Melody was on his knees, now, and he looked up from the prostrate body of the boy with a raised gun and a piercing look to meet this next enemy. The waved hand of the girl warned him first, and then he recognized the pinto which he had given to her, and by that help he knew the girl herself.

But he gave her not a glance after that. She arrived and threw herself from the saddle in time to be received with curt, quick commands to hold this—to pull there—to help here! For Melody, his face whiter than the face of his victim, was slashing the body of Slim out of its clothes, and presently the scrawny torso of Slim appeared with a small purple blotch in the chest. Melody raised and turned the body gently—in the rear of the body, below the shoulder blades, there was a great gaping hole through which the bullet had torn its way out.

Juanita, turning sick, braced herself against a rock, but harsh orders came barking at her ears. Melody was working in desperate haste to make a bandage. Out of his shirt and that of the boy he constructed it, passing it round and round the slender chest, and Juanita, presently, was working swiftly beside him. When that was done, he gave a small swallow of brandy to Slim, and the eyes of the youngster fluttered open for an instant of recognition.

"Oh, Lord, Melody," said he, with a smile of admiration, "you're fast. But next time—I'll get you—sure—"

His voice trailed away. His eyes closed again, and Melody, still supporting the meager body in his arms, looked sternly across to the girl.

"And you," he snapped out. "What are you doing here?"

Oh, to ride those many weary leagues to make an effort so great with all one's heart, and then to be greeted in such a fashion!

She looked down for a moment, biting her lip; then she swallowed her grief and drew out the three emeralds and showed them to him with a look of hope.

"Do you see, Luis? They are worth more than all the money you took from the bank. And when that is paid, my father says that you can come back and face all of the other charges. Do you understand that, Luis? And why do you look at me with such a black face? What have I done?"

He pointed mutely to her clothes.

"How else could I dare to come—alone?" said she.

And at this, he made a gesture to the sky. "Do you know how they'll handle you in their talk?" he asked her fiercely. "Do you know how they'll mark you with soot? But we can't talk about it now. There's something more important, and that's the life of this little fool—or hero—God knows which he is. Juanita, he's dying, I think, unless he can have better care than I can give him. Ride, girl! Ride as though your horse were on wings. I've got to stay here with him and do what I can. Take the Gray Pacer. He's like a lamb, now. Only don't touch him with the spurs. He'll fly with you all the way. Here—I'll shorten the stirrups! Now go! And go fast! Never draw the rein on him. Hills are nothing to him, but kill him to get to Elkhorn. Find a doctor—keep my name away from him if you can—and bring him back on the fastest horse he can get. Do you understand?"

She was in the saddle, now.

"But if they recognize Gray Pacer—if they follow—if they take you, Luis—"

"What does that matter? But I'm not taken until—"

"I shall not go!" cried the girl. "Not until I have your word to make no fight if they come in on you—not until I have your word to surrender, Luis—and to take these things to pay—"

She forced the emeralds into his hand.

"Take your father's charity? Great heavens, Juanita, do you think I'm such a begging cur? No—"

A groan from the wounded boy cut him

short and was echoed by another cry from Lew Melody:

"I'll promise everything. But ride now! If he dies, I'm damned forever. There's no place in hell hot enough for me!"

EIGHTEEN

No sooner had Doctor Loren Kennedy closed his office door and settled himself to a cigar which was rather above the price he usually afforded, than he heard a clattering of hoofs in the street and then a small whirlwind of a boy darted through the door—a wonderfully handsome, graceful boy, crying out: "Are you Doctor Kennedy?"

"There's an accident—a gun—" said Kennedy with a gloomy foreboding.

"There's a dying boy in the hills!" said Juanita. "And—"

But here, through the open door, he saw the glorious form of the Gray Pacer, now darkened and shining with sweat.

"The Gray Pacer!" breathed the honest doctor. "Youngster, what has Lew Melody to do with this?"

"Nothing!" said Juanita, twisting her

hands together in an ecstasy of haste. "But hurry—he's shot through the body—"

"By Lew Melody!" insisted the doctor. "Tell me the truth, or I don't stir a foot!"

"God forgive you if harm comes to him!" said Juanita. "Yes, it is Lew Melody."

Loren Kennedy lost himself for a single instant in thought, but then he knew the thing which he must do. He told her to remount the horse, and then he ran for his own horse shed, but on the way he waved to his man of all work, who was digging in the vegetable garden. It brought the fellow thumping after him, and while the doctor saddled his best horse, he gasped out instructions.

"I'm riding into the hills to take care of a man whom Lew Melody has wounded. Lew himself will probably be there. The moment we've started on, get out into the street and stop every man you find to tell them the news. Tell them to trail us. Tell them to ride hard. I don't know, but I think that this day may be the last free day for Melody, and if it is I'll see that you share my part of the reward."

I have used that instance a hundred times since, in my sermons, to prove the power of money, which works silently and unrelentingly to accomplish the work of its possessor. I have no doubt that Doctor Kennedy was as moral and as just a man as most, but, nevertheless, the pressure of the eternal dollar carried him off his feet at just the right moment to bring peril to Lew Melody.

But, indeed, it hardly needed his warning to bring other riders instantly behind them. For when they started down the street, half a dozen had already gathered to see the Gray Pacer. Even with this seeming boy on his back, the horse was too well known and too much talked about to go unnoticed or unrecognized. And the whir of comment went like lightning through the town. An unknown boy, riding the Gray Pacer, had come into the village and gone off with Doctor Kennedy, both riding as if they were possessed. What could be the meaning of that, unless Lew Melody lay wounded or ill among the mountains, in such a desperate need that he had sent this youngster in on the famous horse to rush out succor to him?

In the meantime, the two rushed their mounts through the rough trails by which the girl had come down to the town, and as they galloped over down slopes and level, and as they struggled up sharper ascents, the doctor ever and anon turned his head and pried at his companion with a piercing glance. Before they reached the Culver Cut his suspicions were running very high indeed. And when she saw what was in his face, the first blush was enough to confirm them. It was a wretched ride for Juanita Cordoba, on this day; and shame was hot in her, and anger at the cold impertinence of this doctor. Truly, he must have been a man without many of the graces and without much kindness in his heart!

However that might be, he was a man of worth in his own profession, and when they swept into view of the wounded boy, the doctor was already loosening the strap which secured his medical kit.

The doctor truly landed working, and he was instantly upon his knees and laboring over the prostrate boy.

"Is there hope," was the first question of the outlaw, as he instinctively obeyed the directions of the doctor in lifting and turning the body of the boy.

"I don't know," said Kennedy.

Then: "Doctor, if you don't need me, I

171

shall have to ride on. You will understand why!"

Of course the doctor understood why, and of course that was the reason that he lied broadly but smoothly enough, because he wished to detain Melody until his capture might be sure. For the reward had been pushed to seventy-five hundred dollars since the taking of the Gray Pacer.

"Man," he said to Lew, "I'm helpless without you. Do as you think best, but if you leave me I shall not answer for the life of this boy."

And Lew, with a groan, and one longing look up the Culver Cut, where he knew he should be riding for life by this time, submitted.

He added with a sudden thought: "Doctor Kennedy, I want you to know the Señorita Juanita Cordoba!"

The doctor turned upon her with a broad grin and a bold eye. "I had my own idea!" said he.

But the sharp voice of Lew Melody—how well I know that voice!—brought him up with a jerk on the curb.

"I have a hope that this lady is to be my wife, Doctor!"

The tone and the message both were

enough to make the doctor bite his lip and turn crimson, and he nodded to the girl; then he went back to his work. He was so busy that Lew Melody could turn to the girl with a gesture as much as to say: "If not this—you are hopelessly compromised! Am I right?"

And she, throwing out her hands to him behind the doctor's back, was saying with her trembling lips: "Do you love me, Don Luis?"

"With all my heart!" lied Lew Melody, like a gentleman.

Here the eyes of the boy popped open.

"I heard the whole thing," he muttered faintly. "Jimminy, Lew, you don't mean it, though! He ain't a girl!"

"*He* is!" said Lew Melody, smiling.

"Oh, Lord!" said the boy. "What have I said to her—and how've I treated her— Oh, *Lord!* What'll she think of me?"

"Nothing but good," said Lew Melody. "Nothing but good."

"Aw," said Slim, "when I think—"

"Hush!" said the doctor. "You must not talk!"

"Steady, partner!" said the more gently warning voice of Melody.

"Shut up, doc," answered the irrepressible Slim. "Look here, old-timer," he added to Melody, "I ain't gunna bump out. I ain't gunna go dark. I could carry around ten slugs like them. Only—"

Here he closed his eyes and his face wrinkled with a spasm of pain. But after that, he looked up eagerly toward Melody.

"I pretty near sneezed," said he, full of anxious apology for this contortion of the face. "Ground kind of damp, maybe!"

"Maybe," said Lew gravely.

"And they's another thing, Lew. Maybe this here bone sawer will be follered along by some of his pals. Beat it, Lew, will you? For the Lord's sake beat it before they nab you—"

"Will you shut your mouth!" snarled out the doctor. "Before that wound starts bleeding again—"

But it was too late to give a warning to Lew Melody. He looked up and down the valley, now, and he saw with one sweep of his eyes that his fate was coming upon him. They had not ridden out of Elkhorn in the form of a few stragglers. Two score hardy men had pushed into the hills, and ten had been outridden by their more luckily mounted companions. Now, spreading out like a fan and converging rapidly toward the mouth of the little ravine in which the boy was lying with Lew near, they spurred along at full speed.

For an instant Lew thought of the last great chance and started to his feet. But the ravine walls before him were almost as sheer as masonry, and his foes were coming fast. He merely unbuckled his belt and laid it beside Slim.

"Keep that, Slim," said he. "Because you're the chief winner."

And Slim, cocking up his head with an agonizing effort, saw the approaching horsemen and lay back with a groan.

"Aw, what a coyote I am, Lew!" said he.

NINETEEN

The men of Deputy Sheriff Marston's party were at least useful for bringing back the fugitive; and there were additions to the escort. It was felt that eight men were hardly enough to form a safe bodyguard for such a desperado as Lew Melody. And, in fact, had I been in Marston's place, I know that I should have welcomed an escort of a hundred.

175

And I shall never forget the face of Lew Melody as he came in this fashion back to his home town. One might have thought, from his appearance, that he was returning from a pleasant jaunt—unless it were because of the shackles on his hands, and the manner in which his horse was tethered to the horse of Marston. But he carried his head as high as ever, and turned it from side to side to view the staring faces which lined the street and crowded the porches. There was perfect calm and perfect contempt in his manner, so that Mrs. Cheswick, though she was not a harsh-minded woman, burst out to me: "Doesn't he *look* like a killer?"

And though I would not admit it aloud, I could not help admitting it to myself. For such demoniacal pride must ride to the ruin of others, I felt.

We crowded like sheep after the procession and saw the cavalcade stop in front of the jail and saw the heavy doors opened, and saw Lew Melody march up the steps with Joe Crockett beside him and Marston behind.

The meeting between Crockett and Lew became famous.

"Well, Lew," said Crockett, "I'm glad

to see you back. But I ain't gunna forgive you for turnin' down my hoss for another nag!"

I went to Joe Crockett at once and asked him if I might see the prisoner; but before I had half finished my request, there was a sudden silence among the people who had been chattering outside the door; and then in came none other than Sandy Furnival. She was pale, but there was a spot of excitement in each cheek, and if she were changed a little in outward appearance, the spirit of Sandy could never change, and that was beautiful to the last. She spoke to me with a smile, and then to Joe Crockett: "I wonder if you will let me see Lew Melody, Mr. Crockett."

I can answer that I, for one, grew weak and faint; and Joe Crockett had to clear his throat twice before he could speak.

"Right this minute, Sandy," said he. "Come along with me."

So he led her into the nest of cells and brought her to Lew Melody.

Half a hundred people heard what was said, for voices carried loudly in that barn of a place and through the thin walls; neither did either of them care to speak in whispers. And she said to him instantly:

"Lew, I've come to tell you that I've changed my mind. I used to be very proud, I think. But I have no pride left. I love you, and I want you; and if I've been cold to you, Lew, it was only because my heart was breaking. Will you believe me?"

Who could have heard her without belief? Not the sheriff and not I, as we leaned shamelessly against the door of his office to hear what we could. We gripped one another. And the sheriff was whispering: "Lord, Lord, will you listen to that? Will you listen to that?"

Then he heard Melody say in such a voice as I have never heard before or since, there was such an agony in it: "I've asked Juanita Cordoba to be my wife, if I come alive out of this thing, Sandy."

And a little breath of silence after that; only the sheriff's whispered curses could I hear.

But Melody added: "But I'll never come out of it, Sandy; and I hope to heaven that I don't. I'm weary of living!"

"Hush!" said Sandy. "Isn't that a weak, silly thing to say? But you *will* come out of it, Lew. Besides, you'll be happy with—"

"Sandy!"

"I won't say it, then," said she.

"Sandy, will you tell me that you'll try to understand?"

"I *do* understand," said she, with never a quaver of her voice. "It's the only right thing, and the just thing. It was she who went to you!"

What a dying note of bitterness in her tone as she said that!

"But always, and now, and ever after, if I live—there's nothing under God to me except your love, Sandy!"

But she? To this day the wonder of her and the scorn of myself and all other men burns up in me when I remember it.

She said in a clear voice as she paused at the outer door: "Will you tell Mrs. Cheswick that I'll be in again for the next choir rehearsal, Mr. Travis?"

I tried to speak; I suppose that I did say something; but it was not intelligible to my own ear, and then we heard the click of the door which told us that she was gone.

The trial had to hang fire for some weeks, because the star witness was not able to appear—that star witness being, of course, Slim. In the meantime, opinion in the valley was divided under two heads. Before the return of Lewis Melody, there had been only the one camp, and this was crowded with his whole-hearted enemies. But now there were two great parties, and the majority were those who upheld the cause of Lew with a sentimental violence. I do not blush to state that I was one of the leaders of this faction. I rejoice to say that Joe Crockett was next to me in the violence with which he upheld the side of the outlaw.

On the other side, the minority were a little more compactly organized than ours, I must admit. But I think it is generally true that benevolent emotions are usually dissipated in talk, whereas malice works with edged tools.

Upon this occasion, Bert Harrison came in from his ranch and got himself a great deal of notoriety by strongly advocating the prosecution of Lewis Melody in the bitterest fashion.

As for the defense, it was baffling to discover that while rich Cordoba was breaking his heart with eagerness to spend tens of thousands to get the finest lawyer in the land for this case, Lew Melody himself refused to retain special counsel and insisted that a young lawyer whom the judge appointed was quite good enough to represent his affairs!

In the meantime, the lesser charges had fallen by the boards. Joe Crockett refused to prosecute any charges of resisting arrest or assault on an officer of the law; and thereby Crockett gained an almost unanimous election the next time that he ran. As for the bank robbery, old Cordoba took a trip north and saw the bank officials at Comanche Crossing, with the result that that charge was squelched. There remained only the Geary affair. And yet that was really the one great thundercloud which would have made all of the other charges seem ridiculous in comparison.

Well, to come to an end to this portion of the narrative, the trial began. And, in the beginning, the evidence for the prosecution seemed very damning. For the gold of Bert Harrison had placed a very competent lawyer at the elbow of the district attorney, and the cross-questioning to which they subjected Lew Melody was very severe and pointed.

He was a poor witness for himself. He answered any question and answered it almost at random; indeed, he began to contradict himself on small points. And it went to such an extent that the impression suddenly gathered head through the court-room and through the mind of the judge and of the twelve jurors, that Lew Melody did not greatly care whether or not he lived or died!

This, from a lad of twenty-two, was very odd. And yet there was a confirma-tory and explanatory rumor. The whole town knew the pitiful details of the last interview between Sandy and Lew—the whole town except the Cordoba family, I dare say. And every day there were the Cordobas, sitting all three in a pale, anx-ious row, worshiping Lew Melody with their eyes, and Juanita growing whiter from day to day. But, on the other hand, when people looked for the face of the other girl, they found only the grim, set features of Mr. Furnival, who sat always in the same place, seeing and hearing everything and watching with a sort of remorseless scorn everything that went on.

When the defense began, it had very little to go upon. The testimony of Lew Melody on his own behalf was extremely poor. He merely would say that he had met Geary under the shadow of a great oak and that they had fought it out. And he freely admitted that he had rushed out of the Furnival house with the announced intention of finding and killing Stan Geary.

When all of this had been established, to the comfort of the prosecution and the utter confusion of Lew's young lawyer, there was a call for Slim.

Never had such a witness taken the stand.

"What other name?" asked the clerk. "What real name, your honor, if you please?"

"What real name?" said the judge to Slim.

"The devil," said Slim. "How do *I* know?"

Which brought a roar, and made the court turn purple to keep from exploding. He had already struck a snag when, in swearing the witness and asking him if he would swear—

"Sure," broke in Slim, "I'm an old hand at it."

If the proceedings were almost broken up by these replies, it was certain that the impression which Slim made upon the jurors was immensely favorable. They beheld him with twelve enormous grins, nudging one another freely and even whispering behind their hands. For Slim, after all, was known as the boy who had masqueraded as a man for the sake of Lew Melody. And having gone out to kill, and having been nearly killed instead, was it not remarkable to see him turn with a broad smile of welcome to the prisoner at the bar, and sing out most informally: "Hello, Lew. I'm gunna help you get out of the mess!"

I skip the first questions. They were not of importance until Slim began to detail events of his life with Geary. And, in spite of objections, Slim was able to rattle out certain details of the manner in which Geary had treated him, and every man in the courtroom grew fighting mad, and every woman grew rosy with anger.

So, when the stage was set, the young lawyer for the defense began to snap out questions concerning a certain night on which Slim had gone to bed early—"because Geary kicked me in the ribs and it sort of tired me!"

And he had fallen asleep in the dirty, dark attic, when he was awakened by the sound of voices below.

At this point, a person of no less importance than Bert Harrison was seen to rise with a pale face and hurry out of the courtroom.

"And whose voices were they?" asked the lawyer.

"One was Geary, of course, and the other was a gent that called himself Bert Harrison!"

Considering the sudden exit of Bert Harrison, this brought every one up erect.

"And what did they talk about?"

"Harrison was offering two hundred dollars to Geary for the murderin' of my partner, yonder—Lew Melody! But Geary, he held out for five hundred, and he got it!"

The prosecution, in vulgar language, curled up and died upon the spot. There remained of it hardly more than a dust streak on the face of the world. And, since all the other charges had been dropped, Lew Melody was set free in fairly record time, and had his hand wrung by twelve good men and true, and by the judge in person, and by all of Barneytown which could get near enough to do it.

But it seemed to please him no more than if they had been wooden images. He was engulfed by the Cordobas and taken away by them, through the town, and over the rickety bridge, past the danger line, and to their house.

As for Bert Harrison, he disappeared for some time. There was no pressure of the charge against him, but life would not have been agreeable to him in our community after that, and perhaps he was wise to leave his affairs altogether in the hands of lawyers.

TWENTY

It was a few weeks later when a panting youth ran through the door of Cordoba, the moneylender. "Don Luis—" he gasped out in a trembling voice.

Cordoba rolled with surprising rapidity to his feet. "What of Don Luis?" he cried. "Adios, adios, señor! I am very busy, as you see!"

And the prospector, feeling that he had just been in the midst of a happy dream, hurried out into the day to make sure that this generosity was not in fact the stuff that dreams are made of.

"Now you speak of my son, of Don

Luis!" cried the moneylender to the youngster. "What is there to say of him?"

"May he always be fortunate," gasped out the boy, recovering his breath as fast as he might. "But I have just heard through my cousin that Miguel and Cristobal Azatlan—"

"What are they?"

"It was a year ago, señor, that Don Luis met with their brother, a very famous fighter from Mexico—"

"And killed that man?"

"Yes."

"Quick, boy! And tell me if they have come to revenge his death?"

"It is that—set!"

Cordoba wrung his fat hands. "The Lord bring them to a wicked end!" cried he. "But now, boy, do not let a word of this come to the ears of Señor Don Luis Melody."

"Señor Cordoba, will you not warn him?"

"Warn him?" echoed Cordoba. "Name of heaven, no!"

"But they are dreadful fighters! Miguel Azatlan on a day in Juarez—"

"Do not tell me! Do not tell me! Foolish boy, do you not know that the more dreadful they are, the more my son will wish to meet them?"

But Cordoba straightway locked his office securely and mounted a horse strong enough to bear up his weight, but passive enough to suit his rather timorous temper; it was a sort of rough plow horse which jogged with him through the twisting alleys of the Mexican quarter, and over the rickety bridge, which was known as the danger line, and so arching above the waters of the yellow Barney River into the American section of the village on the eastern bank. He went straight to the jail, and there he found Sheriff Joe Crockett. He tumbled at once into his story.

"Señor Crockett, you are a good friend to my Don Luis."

"D'you mean Lew Melody?" barked out the sheriff, who was in a rough humor. "And why in the devil should I be a good friend to him—me with my right arm workin' like a rusty gate since he sent that slug of lead through my shoulder?"

Cordoba blinked at him, and then made out the note of friendly raillery which had underlain the speech.

"A bullet or two will not make a difference between two American friends," said he, grinning. "But you pour out a little blood as we would pour out a little wine. Is it not so?"

"Aw," said the sheriff, "I dunno about that. What's eating you today?"

"Your good friend, and my son, Don Luis—"

"Hey! Has he married Juanita?"

"Not yet—the next week—"

"Then don't call him your son until after the marriage. Go on!"

"Two cruel fighting demons have come up from Mexico. It happens that they had a wicked brother who met Señor Melody a year ago, and they have kept a vengeance in their hearts all this time. Now they have come to Barneytown—they have arrived today—"

"Well," said Joe Crockett, "what of that?"

"What of that, señor? You do not wish the murder of your friend?"

Joe Crockett merely smiled, and there was a great deal of sourness in it. "I could go to that pair—what's their name?"

"Miguel and Cristobal Azatlan."

"I could go to 'em if they'd listen to reason and give 'em some ripping good advice to get back to Mexico while they

189

still got whole skins. But if they've come all this way, it'll take more'n talk to turn 'em back. There ain't a thing that I can do except to let Lew Melody go ahead and put on his specialty show—which is out-shooting the shooters, you might say! That's all I can do, Cordoba."

And Joe Crockett did not smile. I think that if there was one man in the valley whose honesty and simplicity could be trusted without cavil, it was none other than this old Mexican moneylender. But Cordoba went back across the river with his worries, and Joe Crockett came to tell me the news.

"They ain't had their lesson yet," was his way of phrasing it. "They're still drifting up the valley to get Lew Melody. Well, in a couple of days there'll be another funeral on the far side of the danger line."

I asked him what he meant, and he explained. I was shocked, naturally.

For my part, I would have been unable to advise him. I felt simply helpless, and so did every one else. But, in the meantime, the suspense grew more tremendous every day, for by a common concurrence of opinion, every one agreed that something was sure to happen before the marriage took place—and now the marriage was less than a week away!

I had barely turned from the gate where the sheriff had spoken to me, when I saw, coming up the street, the man who had filled most of my thoughts for so many weeks. It was Lew Melody himself, but so changed in his costume that I could hardly recognize him at first, in spite of the fact the Lew and only Lew could be riding on the back of the Gray Pacer.

But as that glorious creature, made of modeled silver and shining light, came gliding up the street, turning his beautiful head from side to side to observe and scorn the people he passed, I saw that his rider had transformed himself, in all respects, into a typical Mexican gallant. And I knew that the first chapter of the final drama had been already written!

No one other than Lew Melody would have had the courage to conceive of such a thing, let alone the daring and the sublime scorn of public opinion to execute it. He had been famous through most of his life for the ragamuffin carelessness with which he dressed. A hat or no hat; old rusty boots, blue jeans, a flannel shirt with half the buttons missing, open at the throat, and a ragged pair of gloves—such had been the attire of the Lew Melody who had grown up terrible and careless and gay and wonderful in Barney Valley.

But behold him now, clad in the peaked sombrero of a Mexican youth, with a great band of glittering open gold work surrounding the crown—an open jacket which blazed with gold and silver lace—a shirt of brilliant blue silk—a great crimson sash with great hanging fringes about his waist, and tight trousers buttoned down his leg with immense silver conchos to ornament them. The saddle was a mass of heavy metal work, a staggering cost—the bridle was a jeweler's masterpiece!

But oh, how my heart sank when I saw it! For I could see, I thought, something of things which had passed in the mind of poor Lew Melody before he made this decision.

When he saw me, he waved his hand to me and dismounted. Gray Pacer followed behind his master and stood looking over the shoulder of Lew at me with glittering eyes such as only a stallion, of all the Lord's creatures, possesses.

But here was Lew Melody, not so greatly

changed that he would not do as he had always done out of respect to me—that is, take off his sombrero and stand with it in his hand while he talked. It was a little thing, I suppose, but from this famous youth it cause a tingle to pass through my blood without fail.

I could not help saying, at once: "Ah, Lew, you are going masquerading, are you?"

"I look like it, don't I?" said Melody. "But no—I'm simply stepping into a new name!"

"A new name?" said I.

"I couldn't go on being plain Lew Melody," said he. "Not while my father-in-law-to-be is spending so much money to set me up as a gentleman. I suppose that you've heard about the ranch he's bought for me?"

"Of course I've heard that. It's a splendid place, I understand. I congratulate you, Lewis."

"Don Luis," he corrected again. "Or Luis, at least. Well, it's a very fine place, of course. How many hundreds of acres there are in it I don't know. And how much the timber alone is worth is hard to calculate. But there are three little streams

193

running through it, so that we'll never be bothered by droughts such as this year. I'll be entirely secure there!"

There was an undercurrent of scorn and self-contempt in all of this which I pretended not to see.

"It must have cost a great deal," said I.

"More money than I dare to guess," said Lew Melody. "But Señor Cordoba seems to think nothing of it. The fortune of that man seems to be a staggering thing. He has rivers of gold running into his coffers every day. He simply emptied a few gallons out of his reservoir, and the place was his. But that's not the end of his spending. It's hardly the beginning of it, as a matter of fact. There is the house, too! Nothing but hewn stone for that house, sir!"

"So I have heard."

"Juanita is to be like the fairy princess out of the storybook," he went on. "There are so many yards of lace that it seems to me all the hands in the world, working forever, could never have contrived the stuff. But that's not all. The jewels, sir! It blinds me only to think of them! It really does! Emeralds—rubies—diamonds—what would a marriage be without jewels? And then the pearls! Oh, ropes and strings and heaps of them. Why, I could talk to you about these things through the entire day."

But the next word from him was a sudden whisper.

"Have you seen her lately, sir?"

I did not have to ask whom he meant. "I've seen her," said I.

"Is she well?" asked Lew Melody huskily.

"I think—quite well," I managed to stammer.

"I rode out like a thief in the night," said Melody, "and I peeked through the window at her. I thought she was a little pale. But she is not ill?"

"No, Lewis, not ill."

"Sometimes I wonder—" he began, and then stopped.

I did not ask him to continue, but, as quickly as I could, I changed the subject back to himself.

"A year ago you fought with a Mexican named Azatlan."

"Did I?" said he carelessly. "Yes, I think I did. A dog who tried to knife me in the back."

"You killed him, Lewis."

"I'm glad I was lucky enough to!"

"Two of his brothers are across the danger line, waiting to find you. Will you promise me to be careful?"

"Careful of the life of the son of Señor Cordoba, the rich moneylender?" said he. "Can you ask me such a question? If I did not trouble about myself, I should at least have to take care of such clothes as these, should I not?"

But when he leaped onto the back of Gray Pacer, the direction in which he rode was straight back toward the river, and I knew, then, how well he would heed my warning!

TWENTY-ONE

It seemed as though serious thoughts rolled very easily off the fat, round back of Cordoba; or perhaps it was the sense of his own trouble that brought to his mind the trouble of another.

He said suddenly: "It is the end of that poor Señor Furnival!"

The glance of Juanita flashed whiplike to the face of Lew Melody; if she spoke never of the passion which had taken her lover from her side to that of Sandy Furnival, not so many weeks before, it was not because she did not think of it constantly. Think she did, and now her look probed at the face of Lew Melody. If it had been I, she would have surprised me, I know, in the midst of an expression of dismay which would have told a great deal. But I have noticed that men who are quick with their hands are, also, usually quick with their minds. So that the instant that Lew heard that word, he felt the prick of the spur and then banished all semblance of pain from his face and presented an unruffled brow to Juanita's searching eyes. The señora, too, had looked askance at him; but she discovered no more than did her daughter.

"What's happened to Furnival?" asked Melody, in a matter-of-fact voice.

"He is sick?" asked Juanita.

"He is sick in the purse," said the moneylender, and he could not help smiling a little when he thought of his own comfortable thousands in the bank.

"That's odd," said Melody cheerfully, "because he seemed to be a thrifty man."

"Ah, yes, very thrifty," said the moneylender. "But these thrifty men sometimes forget one little thing—cash, cash, cash! That is it!" He rubbed his hands together and chuckled with self-satisfaction.

"But he has a good ranch," said Lew.

"So-so. It is a good ranch, stocked with good cattle. But there is a mortgage, eh?"

"It is worth more than the mortgage, surely!" said the señora. "I have seen that place. It is good."

"Buying and selling," said the man of money, "is a beautiful thing. Do you know what the generals say? There is a time to fight and a time not to fight. And there is also a time to sell and a time to buy. Well, my children, this is not the time for Señor Furnival to sell. It is very wrong! But he needs cash—cash—cash!"

"The bank—" began the señora.

"It is the bank that holds the mortgage. It is the bank that wants the ranch. You see how beautiful it is?"

"Is the Barneytown bank the only one in the valley?"

"They are all allies," said Cordoba. "And the Barneytown bank has said to the others: Let us alone. We want this thing. Another time, we will keep our hands off when you wish a thing. So it goes, do you see? Señor Furnival gets no money; he must sell; and the bank is the buyer—oh, very cheap! Because no one outside of the banks has the cash—no one except Cordoba!"

"Then why does he not come to you?" asked the wife.

"Who can tell?" said Cordoba, with a grin of satisfaction. "To some, I am only a peon!"

"Father!" cried Juanita, turning crimson.

"Oh, do not look at Luis," said the moneylender. "He knows what fools say of me! But when Furnival does not come to me, should I go to him?"

Juanita glanced again at Lew Melody; he was merely rolling one of his incessant cigarettes, and his face was as calm as the face of a sphinx.

"Ah, Luis," said the girl, "can you be so heartless, when those people were once your friends? Can you see them go down to a great poverty, perhaps, when a word from you would persuade my father?"

Heaven can tell how the heart of Lew Melody must have leaped when he heard this suggestion, but he knew his part, and he merely said: "They are nothing to me. Let these business men take care of their business. Why should your father lose money to help this rancher?"

"Ah, well," said Cordoba, cocking his head upon one side as another phase of the thing entered his mind. "It would be a good loan. It would be—let me see—twelve—perhaps fifteen thousand dollars. One cannot place such loans—at a right interest—every day. But—should I go to him? No. I would lose two per cent simply by asking him for his business. That would be a fool's trick. I am growing old; but I have not grown foolish. No, no!"

I have always seen a fate in this thing—that Juanita should have urged on a matter which ended in her own destruction. But at that moment there was nothing in her saving a great gentleness. And when she looked at Lew Melody and considered her great happiness, she had a consuming pity for all who might be sad in this world.

She said: "Let Luis go to them and talk for you. It would be business from you; it would seem mere friendship from him!"

The moneylender, not displeased, grinned broadly upon his wife. "Is she not my daughter?" said he. "Yes, and she has a head. She has understanding, I tell you!

Well, Luis, will you go to him from me? Will you go to him as a friend?"

I suppose that Lew Melody felt this thing was a gift from heaven, but he pretended to be disinclined.

"It is a long ride, and a hot day," said he. "I should think that a letter would do well enough."

"Luis!" cried Juanita. "Do you mean it?"

"Well," said he, "will it please you if I go?"

"Ah, yes!"

"These good people," said the artful Melody, with a sigh, "make us bad ones work hard to please them. I'll ride to the Furnival ranch if you wish, Juanita."

"Dear Luis!"

"Tush!" said the moneylender. "This may be a good business stroke for me. But look—because it is the wish of Juanita, I shall be generous. There happens to be much money lying idle in my safe. Why should it not work? So I will give them a banker's rate—at six per cent. Now, there is generosity, Luis!"

"Foolish generosity!" said Melody.

"Well, I shall be softhearted for once. But go quickly, Luis. I am eager to learn what he says. Unless he is a madman—go quickly! There is much money idle in my safe! Tell him—it can be arranged by mail, if he cannot take this trip to see me."

It was in this manner that Melody was persuaded to do the thing which lay the nearest to his heart—by the girl and by her father. In the light of things to come, you will see if this was not the work of a controlling Providence which had a care for the sorrows of poor Sandy Furnival.

So, sauntering idly, for fear lest haste on his part might excite the suspicions of the Cordobas, after all, Lew Melody went down to the street to the Gray Pacer, and there he found a down-headed roan mustang with both ears dropping lazily forward, enjoying a sun bath. And, in the meager shadow of his neck, sitting cross-legged in the dust, his back reclining against the forelegs of the little beast, sat a bareheaded boy of fifteen with a young-old face. He was blowing on a harmonica, his eyes half closed in enjoyment of the weird strains which he brought forth.

"Slim!" said Lew Melody, and ran for him.

But Slim held up one restraining hand. "Listen here," said Slim, with a corner of

202

the instrument still in his mouth. "If this ain't swell harmony, I'm a goat!" And he repeated the last strain.

"You'll be a violinist," said Lew Melody. "That's fine!"

At this, a gleam of satisfaction crossed the features of the ragged, dusty boy. He stood up and held out his hand.

"Hello, Lew," said he. "How's things?"

"Where the devil have you been?" asked Lew Melody. "And why haven't I heard from you? And what became of the last suit of clothes I got for you?"

"I was rollin' the bones with Arkansas Joe down to El Paso," said the boy, "and he had the doggonedest run of luck that you ever seen. He got his point five times runnin', and when I doubled my bets and staked my new clothes along with the rest of my pile, darned if he didn't crap and get the whole lot! That was luck! What?"

"That was luck," grinned Lew Melody. He thrust a forefinger into the lean paunch of the boy. "When did you eat last, Slim?"

"Leave me be!" said Slim angrily. "My last meal was a fine breakfast."

"What did you have?"

"Roast chicken," said Slim. "Roast chicken done brown, and roast potatoes in the ashes, and coffee that would make you roll your eyes!"

"That sounds enough," said Melody. "Where did you swipe the chickens?"

"Ah, down the line."

"When was it? Yesterday?"

"Naw. The day before."

"Here's a ten-spot. Blow yourself to a real meal again."

"Thanks," said Slim, stowing the coin with a dexterous palm.

"Why did you fade away, Slim? I thought that you'd stay around with me for a while."

"A handout once in a while is all right," declared Slim, "but mooching steady all the time is beggin'. D'you think that I'd be a beggar, Lew?"

"Of course not. How have you been making any money, though? Riding herd a little?"

"Work," explained Slim, "don't agree with me none. It sort of riles up my blood and gets my head to achin'. When I start to workin' I begin to see pictures, and all the pictures is of some place where I ain't. Funny, ain't it?"

"Very queer," said Lew. "But what brought you back just now?"

"I thought I'd blow in for the wedding and the big eats. There'll be big eats, I guess?"

"Oh, yes. More than you can hold."

"I dunno," said Slim. "When I lay myself out to really eat, I can wrap myself around a whole grocery store, pretty near." He stepped closer to Melody. "A bo down the line," said he, "told me about a couple of birds that come up to scalp you. Name of Azatlan. They ought to be in Barneytown right now."

"I've seen one of them," said Lew Melody. "But thanks for letting me know. That's friendly, Slim."

"Aw, it ain't nothin'," said Slim. "Speakin' personal, I been sort of achin' for a scrap. I been practicin' with this right along. Watch!"

With a lightning gesture he conjured a revolver from his clothes and made it disappear on the opposite side of his body. There had been hardly more than a flash of steel in the sun.

"Fine," said Melody. "That's the real stuff. How much time every day?"

"Two or three hours," said Slim. "And then another hour, pullin' and shooting quick." He added with a sigh: "But I ain't so very sure of my stuff yet, Lew. Well, it's comin', though. I remember what you taught me, pretty well. But I get to pulling with the forefinger instead of squeezing with the whole hand, the way you said!"

So, when Lew Melody slipped into the saddle, on the great gray stallion, the boy jumped onto the back of the roan mustang and they started off together, the pacer sliding along like flowing water, and the mustang pounding hard to keep up. They twisted out through the narrow streets of the Mexican quarter of Barneytown, and across the staggering old bridge across the river, and so on through the broader streets of the eastern town. Then up the hills beyond toward the Furnival ranch they went, until the sharply flashing eyes of the boy detected something moving in a course parallel with theirs, on the farther side of the hill up which they rode that moment.

"Lew," said he, "there's a slick bird trailin' us on the far side of the hill!"

TWENTY-TWO

"**D**id you have a glimpse of him?"
"Only the peak of a hat."
"Broad or sharp?"
"A Mexican peak; Lew. Might it be—"
"I'll see," said Lew Melody, and, twitching the stallion to the right, he turned the fine creature into a silver flash of light that drove up the hillside, leaped a fence on the crest, and shot on like a winged thing floating near the ground, to the farther side of the hill, with poor Slim flogging its best speed out of the mustang but falling more and more hopelessly to the rear with every stride.

So sudden was that charge that the rider on the farther hillside was taken quite from the rear and most wholly by surprise. When he jerked his head around, it was only to see Lew Melody already almost upon him and within point-blank range for pistol shooting.

At that range, men took no liberties with Lew Melody, from the Rio Grande to the Cascade Mountains. His work was too swift and far too sure for any comfort. So the man, a lean-faced individual with very long, Indian-straight black hair that jutted out beneath the band of his hat, stopped his horse and waited for Melody to come up. The Gray Pacer was brought to a swerving halt that made him face the other directly. Melody hooked a thumb over his shoulders.

"The road is yonder," said he. "There is no trail here, my friend." He spoke in Spanish, and the other answered sullenly: "I ride where I choose to ride, señor."

"We do not find men by riding cross-country for them," said Melody. "When we wish to meet them, we ride down the roads. Or, better still, we go to their houses and call them to the door and say: 'Defend yourself!'"

"Señor!" exclaimed the Mexican, with a glitter of danger in his eyes.

"Yes, señor," said Melody. "Yes, Miguel Azatlan!"

The guess struck home so sharply, that the other turned a pale yellow with the shock of it.

"You have my name, then?" muttered he.

"I have your name," said Melody. "But you are not a full blood brother to those bull-faced fools—Pedro and Cristobal. You are not?"

"Their father was my father," said the other, more sullen than ever, but more afraid than sullen.

"You have come up here to talk with me concerning the death of Pedro a year ago?" asked Melody.

"I did not say so."

"But I know your thoughts. It must be that we have mutual friends. And now look around you, Miguel. Here are open fields. There is no one near us except the boy, yonder, and he will report the matter fairly and say that it was a fair fight, no matter which of us drops. Why should you not say what you have to say now?"

"I do not know what you mean," said Miguel, a little more yellow than ever. "I have nothing to say."

"Not even six words?" asked Melody contemptuously. And he pointed to the holster at the hip of the Mexican. But Azatlan regarded him in a glowering silence.

"Very well," said Melody. "It is to be in the dark, then, after all." And, turning his horse fairly around, he presented his back to the Mexican and rode away.

At this tempting target, Azatlan gripped his revolver butt. But still his hand brought it only half out. There was something so light in the carriage of Melody, so suggestive of an animal readiness to whirl and shoot and not miss, that he changed his mind and jammed the gun back into the leather cover.

At the hilltop, Slim rejoined his friend, grinning broadly. "I didn't hear nothin'," said Slim, "but I seen plenty. That sap is gunna dream about you, Lew!"

"The rat is a night worker, it seems," said Lew Melody. "He'll try his hand with me when the lights are out. Over yonder is the Furnival ranch, kid. I have to go there by myself. I suppose that you won't be lonely?"

"Me? I keep my company with me," said Slim, and, turning the mustang under the shade of a tree, he slid off and lay flat in the pale-brown grass; the outlandish strains of the harmonica followed Lew Melody down the road a step or two.

He went straight to the ranch house, but when he rapped and waited, his heart in his mouth, it was not the familiar light step of Sandy Furnival that came up to the door, but a trailing noise of slippers. The Chinese cook opened to Lew.

From the pidgin English of the cook, Melody learned that Furnival was superintending the building of a stack of straw behind the winter sheds for the cattle. So, to the sheds went Lew and found Furnival himself on top of the stack, taking two corners of the great square stack while a hired man labored on the other side of the rising pyramid, and a Jackson fork dumped a quarter of a wagon load at a time on top of the pile. It was well sun faded, this straw, and it rose, now, like a rough mound of ivory against a pale sky. On top, half obscured through the smoke of chaff and dust, Lew saw the grim face of Furnival, set with labor and enjoying his task. He thought it characteristic of the man that, with ruin just around the corner of his life, Furnival should be carrying on the routine work of the ranch with such methodical pains.

A little shudder passed through the body of Lew Melody and set all his lean muscles twitching. For the only thing in the world that he feared, I am sorry to say, was hard work!

The business ended as he approached.

The derrick boy turned to stare at him; the teamster on top of his load paused with the ponderous Jackson fork raised in his hands; and Furnival himself advanced to the edge of the stack and shouted down: "What you want, Melody?"

"I want to talk to you."

"About what?" asked Furnival coldly.

It was very irritating to Lew Melody. He came there intent upon being his mildest self, but when one wishes to have a quiet bull terrier, it is not well to bring it near to a growling dog.

"About your own business," snapped out Lew, "if that interests you."

Now, Furnival was a somber fellow, and I suppose that of all the people in the world, the one he was least fond of was this tall, graceful, handsome young man who sat on the back of the famous Gray Pacer and looked up to him from beneath a gaudy Mexican sombrero. However, after he had paused for a moment, he seemed to decide that it would be better to talk than to explode. So he waded over the loose top of the stack, gripped a derrick rope, and slid down.

He came to Melody, wiping the perspiration and the dust out of his eyes and shouting over his shoulder: "Keep on! This ain't no half holiday!"

The derrick-horse driver came to life with a start, the big Jackson fork was fixed and then went groaning up into the air with its dripping load of straw.

Melody was now standing at the head of the stallion.

"What'll you have?" asked Furnival.

"You're in trouble," said Melody, with an equal sharpness.

"I ain't called for a doctor," said the rancher.

"You're about to be broken up small," said Lew, as coldly as ever. "And you know it."

"What might that have to do with you?"

"I haven't come here for your sake. I suppose that you can guess that."

"We ain't gunna argue that point," said Furnival darkly. "Now lemme hear what you got to say. I'm a busy man."

"I've come to find out what money you need to float you through," said Lew Melody, "and offer you a loan—"

I suppose it was a staggering blow to the rancher. In his hard life, he had never received gifts, he had never taken help. But he had moiled and toiled his way to the possession of all that he owned. Help from any one would have been an absolute novelty to him. But help from a man like Melody, whom he considered an enemy, was very strange!

If he felt a shock of surprise at first, it was followed at once by a total suspicion. Things which are too good cannot be real.

"*You* want to offer me a loan?" he asked gravely.

"From Cordoba."

"Ah," grunted Furnival. "From the greaser, eh?"

It was a rough and a pointless insult— seeing that he and the entire valley knew that Lew Melody was contracted to the daughter of the Mexican.

But if the eye of Melody turned to fire, he controlled his anger at once. And Furnival, seeing that effort at self-control, marveled more than ever. For certainly Lew had no saintly repute for patience.

"From Cordoba," said Melody coldly. "I suppose that money from him would help you as much as money from any one?"

"I dunno," muttered Furnival, still peering intently at the younger man to make out some hidden meaning. "I dunno that I foller your drift, son."

"Open your eyes, then, and look sharp. Is there anything that you can't understand? The bank has cornered you—"

"How did you find that out?"

"From Cordoba."

"And now Cordoba wants to corner me the same way? No, Melody; if I'm gunna go bust, I'll let the bank pick my bones. Thank you!"

A veritable saint would have begun to show some emotion by this time, I believe. As for Lew Melody, he was in a white heat.

"I'm making the offer for the last time!" he cried. "Will you take Cordoba's money at six per cent interest, or will you not?"

TWENTY-THREE

It was the crowning shock to Furnival. Naturally it was not the first time he had taken a loan; that was the direct cause of his downfall. But when a rancher borrows, he usually pays very dearly for it. The cattle business is too uncertain to make banks lend gladly. A famine season

215

may ruin the most prosperous rancher; and so the rates run high on cattle money. Now, of all times, Furnival having his back against the wall, money at six per cent was like money donated freely. He glared at Melody, hunting for the joke behind this suggestion, but when he found the eye of the younger man bright and steady, he looked wildly around him, then back again to this minister of grace.

"Lew," said he finally, "this is a funny thing that you're talking about. I'm about down and done for. I suppose that you ain't meaning it when you talk six per cent?"

"Exactly that! You can have what you want at that rate."

"Young feller," said Furnival with a rising voice, "d'you know what I'm in the hole?"

"Only vaguely."

"I needed eighteen thousand dollars before I can hold up my head!"

"Eighteen thousand dollars," said Lew Melody, "is exactly what you may have!" He added: "Or call it twenty thousand, which will leave you some spare money in the bank to work on."

The sun was burning hot, but Furnival

took off his hat and exposed his face as though to a cooling breeze.

"Say it once more—slow and careful!" said he.

And Lew Melody repeated the offer.

"But why in heaven's name will he do it?" cried the rancher.

"He knows that your ranch is worth it."

"Ay—it is!" exclaimed Furnival. "And more, too. And if I can meet the bank, I'll be so far ahead by the end of the season that I could pay off the whole eighteen thousand. I got my hands on gold—a regular mine—everything is busting my way—except for cash, and the lack of cash was killing me! But now—why I'd be free, Melody!"

"Cordoba is not a fool," said Lew. "He wouldn't lend the money if he didn't know that you were worth it."

"It ain't him," said Furnival. "It's you, Melody, that's doin' this for me!"

"I tell you, it's not, Furnival. I give you my word—"

"You're lyin' to me," snapped the rancher. "It's you that persuaded him. Whoever heard tell of a moneylender sending out beggin' to make a loan—and at six per cent! Why, it's not more than charity, Melody!"

Nothing else could have torn through the outer shell of his strength so effectually, for there was nothing else that Furnival so understood as he understood money and money matters. This was an eloquence of dollars and cents that went to his soul.

And, while Lew Melody persisted that there was no charity in it, and that it was a matter of the sheerest business, Furnival took him by the arm and said: "We're gunna walk into the house where we can talk more comfortable."

He fairly dragged Lew to the house and up the steps of the veranda through the door. The same door where, not long before, he had met Lew with a shotgun in his hands and a sharp command never to show his face again in the Furnival house. But that was forgotten, now. No, as they entered the living room, he turned about and gripped the hand of Melody.

"I said once that I'd never see you inside my house again, Lew. Well, I was a fool. I didn't know you. I was blind to you! But when a man gives good for bad, the way you're doin' now—why, it makes me want to stand on top of the house and talk to the world about it."

"You'll not tell a soul," said Melody.

"But I shall."

"Furnival, you'd embarrass me."

"Hey, Sandy!"

"For heaven's sake!" breathed Lew, when he heard the name of the girl he loved.

And then her sweet voice from the upper part of the house made answer, and he heard the quick, light step come through the upper hall.

"I can't stay. You mustn't tell her about it," said Lew, completely miserable. "I'm going now. Let me go, Furnival!"

"Let you go? I'll see you damned first!" He laid a gigantic grip upon the arm of Lew. "Hey, Sandy! Will you hurry up?"

Sandy came in a breathless whirl to the open door, and there she stopped short and threw her hand up before her face. For it was a cruel thing to bring her so suddenly into the sight of the man she loved.

But Furnival was in the midst of a speechmaking effort, the first in his life, and the glow of his enthusiasm did not permit him to see the pain and the white shock in the face of his daughter.

"I dragged Lew into the house," said the rancher, "because you got the lingo to talk right to him, and I ain't! I dragged him in here first to tell you that he's saved us, Sandy. Why he done it, I dunno, except that he's naturally white. But here's the work of my life—this here house—that chair and that table—and everything beyond that window, from the straw to the cows—the whole work of my life was gunna go up in smoke, Sandy. And now Lew comes in to save me, after I've treated him like a mangy dog. I say that it warms my heart!"

"No, Sandy," broke in Lew Melody. "I have no money. I could not do it. It is the money of Cordoba, and he deserves the praise."

"You hear him?" laughed the rancher, swelling with joy. "Why, he's modest, too. Darned if I ain't seein' him for the first time. Sandy, are you struck dumb? Ain't you got a word?"

"Bless you, Lew," said Sandy, and went up to him and smiled in his face.

"I'll go see Cordoba and arrange things with him," said Furnival. "You might fix up a snack or something for Lew, Sandy. I'm not gunna be back till the middle of the afternoon at the earliest. So long!"

He was through the door with a rush like the rush of a happy boy. His daughter and her lover remained gravely behind, like old people indeed.

"As soon as he has gone, I'll go," said Lew. "As soon as we hear his horse."

She shook her head. "There's no need of that," said she.

And a heavy silence fell between them, until the rapid clattering of the hoofs of the rancher's horse began and died off down the road. Then Lew Melody picked up his hat and turned toward the door.

He had almost passed through it when a low cry from Sandy stopped him. I wonder what the future might have been for them if that cry had not been uttered. But Melody turned and saw Sandy leaning against the wall very pale and very drawn about the mouth.

"What is it, Sandy?" said he.

"I don't want you to go," said she. "I'm too weak to let you go just now!"

He went back to her and took her cold face between his hands. "Do you think it's right?" said he.

"I don't know," said Sandy. "Is it wrong?"

They were both trembling; they were both pinched of face and great of eye.

"Only I thought—" said Sandy.

"Tell me," said he.

"That it was our last chance for a little happiness together, Lew."

"It *is* our last chance," said he.

I don't like to repeat what was said then by Sandy, but all her heroism vanished and left her weak and all too human. But she cried out: "Ah, my dear, why should she have you? Is it only because she rode a horse up into the hills to find you? Is it that, which gives her the right to have you? But I won't submit to it. I'll fight; because it's my life and my happiness that I fight for! And I love you; and you love me; tell me if you do!"

I am glad that I never had to feel such an agony as went through Lew Melody as he listened to her and stared drearily before him at the wall.

TWENTY-FOUR

Slim had not lain under his tree long when he heard something behind him, no louder than the rushing of a bird's wing through the air, but it made him drop the harmonica and whirl over on his belly with his revolver slipped into his hand by a gesture of wonderful speed such as Lew Melody himself had seen and approved. And when Slim had turned upon his stomach, he found that the barrel of the gun was pointed straight at the piratical form of Miguel Azatlan, who was just half a step from the far side of the tree, sneaking along stealthily with a sort of congealed malice in his face. He stopped with a shock at the sudden change in the posture of the boy. But, after the first start, he was inclined to regard the leveled revolver, in such young hands, as little more than a poor joke. So he grinned at Slim.

"Be careful, my son," said he in Spanish. "There might be a bullet in that!"

"Might there be?" said Slim, showing his teeth as he smiled. "And there might be a pair of 'em—and there might be three

223

pairs, too. And every pair might be meant for you—you yaller-skinned, rat-eyed, long-drawn-out, blue-mouthed alligator!"

"I shall make you yell for that!" said Miguel, turning into a demon at once. "I shall teach one young gringo—"

"Say, greaser," said the boy, "you got a tassel on the side of your hat that you don't need. So I'm gunna take it off for you."

He had his aim on the tassel, well enough, but that aim was a little too close. He clipped off the tassel, but the big-faced bullet tore into the body of the sombrero itself and ripped through the tough felt and sliced away the hatband, and in short, knocked the sombrero so neatly off the head of the Mexican, that it spun away through the air and left him suddenly bareheaded.

He clapped his hand to his bare sconce with a shout of surprise. And then he snatched out a gun only to hear the sharp voice of this evil young American ripping at his ear: "Drop that gun, or I'll salt you, sure!"

Miguel hesitated; then, being lost in fact, he dropped the gun in all obedience and glowered at Slim.

"Young murderer!" he gasped.

A lie began to expand in the fertile brain of Slim, and grow into a rosy dream of fiction. He began to narrate: "Sometimes I lay down by the old Rio and snooze in the bushes. Pretty soon, I hear some sap coming down for water on the far side of the river. Then I up and draw a bead on him and give him a yell. And when he looked up, he got it."

"Son of a devil!" snarled Miguel. "You will be buzzard food before many days— you and Señor Melody. I spit on you and scorn you!"

So he turned himself about and walked away with as much dignity as he could muster. Slim, however, picked up the revolver and gloated over it. It was of a new make, in perfect condition, and all of the six chambers were loaded. The armament of Slim was, in this fashion, doubled on the spot.

However, it was no time for him to linger. Since Miguel had been affronted in this fashion, there was not much which he would not attempt, and there were too many ways of getting, unperceived, within at least rifle range of this tree. So Slim gathered up the reins of Sam, the mustang, and jumped on his back to find a new resting place.

But, as he did so, he heard a clattering of hoofs. He knew that it was not Lew Melody coming down the road, for the sound of the Pacer's rhythmic tread was unmistakable to his sharp ears, so he waited with some curiosity.

What he saw, breaking around the bend of the hill and beating up a cloud of dust from the road, was none other than Furnival himself. The rancher was riding hard, and though he was on a willing horse, yet its pace did not suit him, and he mended it from time to time with a stinging cut from a quirt, so that the wind of that gallop made the brim of his hat furl up stiffly in front.

That was enough for Slim. He considered that flying figure for one instant and, comparing its gait with the best pace which he could get out of old Sam, he knew that he could never overtake the flying horseman to ask any questions. Yet he was greatly alarmed. He was too well acquainted with the habits of Lew Melody to be surprised by a disaster of any kind worked by his hands.

What first leaped through the brain of

Slim was that Melody might have had trouble with one of the men at the Furnival ranch and that he had shot the man down. Now Furnival himself was rushing for the nearest doctor; that was the meaning, he thought, of such ardent riding on the part of such an elderly and sedate man.

With Slim, as the saying goes, to think was to act. If his idol, Lew Melody, had recently shot down a man, then Lew himself was now in very real trouble. And a man in trouble needs his friends. This was thinking enough for Slim. He turned the roan mustang toward the ranch of Furnival and rode thither at full speed.

But the very first thing that he saw disarmed the greater part of his suspicions. For he discovered that the derrick behind the cattle sheds was still working busily, lifting forkful after forkful of straw to the top of the growing stack, from which a faint smoke of dust and chaff was rising. If there had been a shooting scrape on the place, it seemed most unlikely indeed that the men would be working on in this fashion. If they remained at the stack, it would be to sit in a cluster and talk over similar affairs which had occurred in the valley—particularly if such a person as famous

Lew Melody were concerned in the matter.

So Slim paused and took patient thought before he decided upon his next step. It even occurred to him that he might return to the vicinity of the tree where Lew had left him, but when a boy of Slim's age has decided that something may be wrong, and that it concerns the welfare of a friend, he cannot sit down and fold his hands. In another moment Slim had started for the house of Furnival.

He went to the front veranda, dismounted, and stood a moment at the front door. There was not a sound from the house. And yet Lew Melody was not with the working men, and had not returned to the oak, and was certainly not with Furnival himself, who had ridden so hard in the direction of Barneytown. It began to seem like an exciting mystery to Slim when, far and faint in the house, he heard the sound of a girl's voice, and, a moment later, the familiar murmur of Lew Melody.

It was such an immense relief to Slim that he was about to turn away with a sigh; and then he grew interested, not to eavesdrop upon the pair, but in the nice experiment of seeing how sharply he could attune his ears to those light sounds.

There are ways and ways of listening, but few have the power to throw their attention in a definitely concentrated direction. Yet, from the wide and circling horizon of noises around him, Slim shut out from his consciousness the yelping of a far-off coyote—a mere pulse in the air— the sharper conversations from the hen yard behind the house, the dreary squeaking of the derrick pulley, the lowing of a cow like a doleful horn in the distance—all of these noises were closed out of the ear of Slim, and he heard, only, the delicate stir of voices within the house itself. Then, having shut out all else, as a burning glass focuses the sun to a point of fire, so Slim centered his attention and received a reward. For, at once, he could distinguish the thread of the conversation. The merest puff of wind would have shattered that dainty web of sound, but no wind came, and presently Slim was fascinated by the picture which those voices were painting for him—a picture so startling and so grim that he could not believe the ears with which he heard it. For he had looked upon Lew Melody as the happiest man in the world; and now he could peek behind the curtain and see the truth! Only a brief glimpse of the truth, but that was enough.

"I shall manage in some way," was the first thing Slim heard Sandy saying.

"Ah, Sandy," said Lew Melody, "I wondered why I should be punished like this, but now I can understand. It's because I've lived for myself and hunted for nothing but my own fun—and my fun was making trouble for other people. I've lived by the gun; and now I'm punished for it."

"You'll be happy, Lew."

"I shall be?"

"She is very pretty; and she loves you. And so do all the Cordobas. But how could they help it? And you'll have money. That helps to smooth out life, I know."

"When she came to me like that in the mountains—I had to do something to save her name. Was there anything else?"

"You had to marry her, Lew. It was the only right thing. Do you think that I shall ever reproach you for it?"

"I know that. And it only makes the pain harder to bear."

"Besides, perhaps I shall be happy, too, after a while. There are things for one to do. And my father needs me. I shall find some sort of happiness. But oh, how I wish that I had never broken out at you today! It was only because father brought you in so suddenly—and said so many kind things about you just for a moment I thought that my heart would break. Because I love you so! Do you forgive me?"

Slim tiptoed from the veranda with a white face.

It was much more to him than if he had looked in upon a frightful murder. He was fifteen, and at fifteen the ideals are as rigidly established as lofty walls of steel. So it was with Slim. Here was his pleasant picture of the future life of Lew Melody pulled down around his ears. He had seen him the husband of a lovely girl, the son-in-law of a rich man; trouble seemed annihilated for Melody. But here was the truth! And that a man should marry a woman he did not love, even from a sense of duty, seemed to Slim—thief, vagabond, and incipient gunfighter as he was—the most deadly and blasting of sins.

"Something has got to be done!" said Slim.

TWENTY-FIVE

Such a decision as Slim had come to was proper enough; but what under heaven could be accomplished he did not see so clearly. What he was determined upon, however, was that this false marriage should not take place. It was true that he knew Juanita and liked her very well; but he had seen Sandy also, and to see her, as the poet says, was to love her. Moreover, he felt that this project of Melody, to marry one woman while he truly cared for another, was a crime so dreadful that anything was permissible to prevent it. Therefore means, no matter how brutal, did not appeal to Slim as things to be rejected. His only difficulty was to find the way in which the thing could be done.

In the first place, he decided that he could not endure to meet Melody face to face at once. There would be too great a danger of his tongue running away with his discretion, and Melody must not now suspect what was in his mind; for nothing he could say, he very well knew, could alter the mind of Lew.

So he rode the roan mustang straight

back toward Barneytown, but at a very slow gait; and slowly he was passing through the streets when he came past my house just as I was busy in the garden watering Lydia's hedge of sweet peas, which is the joy of her life, I think, beyond anything else in the world. Well, it is a pretty thing, that hedge, and I think that when it calls the eyes of the townsmen toward our house, it sends them by with a happy thought of their clergyman.

However, the sun was very hot, and when I saw Slim, I was glad to retreat to a corner of the garden under the shade of a tree and turn the hose into the trench to run as it pleased—a thing which Lydia greatly objects to. I waved to Slim, and he rode his horse up close to the fence. He was proud of his ability to talk with men like a man would, and now he drew himself up in the saddle and looked in a patronizing fashion over the brilliant wall of the fragrant color which the sweet-pea hedge raised into the sun. The aroma of it went like a secret blessing half a block away, when the wind was blowing softly.

"That ain't a half-bad garden," said Slim. "But, Jiminy Christmas! Mr. Travis, what a pile of work you and Mrs. Travis must put in on it!"

"Quite a bit," said I. "Quite a bit, but it's worth it. Don't you think so?"

"Well," said this imp, "we all got our own tastes, you know. Speakin' personal, I'd say that these here sweet peas smell pretty sweet, but they smell like work, too, and I dunno that I care for the smell of work."

"Work," said I, a little sententiously I fear, "is the only great happiness in life."

The eyes of Slim opened at me. "Might that be a joke?" he asked, with a frown of wonder on his young-old face.

"Not at all a joke," said I. "Because, you see, man is intended to labor."

Slim blinked. "I dunno that I see that very clear," he admitted.

"Ah, Slim," said I, "who is guilty of giving you an education without any religion?"

"I dunno," said Slim, "whoever done any educating of me, except Lew Melody, with a gun. Maybe he ain't good enough for you?"

He said this with the cold smile of one who names a perfect man and dares criticism to show its face. But I was not in a humor to assail Lew Melody.

"Ah, well," said I, "I would need a great deal of time to convince you. Life will teach you, however. The trouble is that life is a painful schoolmaster. And religion comes easily into the mind of man at two times only—his childhood and his deathbed."

"I'd like to know one thing," said Slim, "and that's this talk about hell. How much real stuff is there in it?"

I could only say: "I don't know. But some of us feel that there must be some punishment hereafter for sins which are not punished on earth. Just as we hope that there is a reward for the good that is done."

"What would you say," said Slim, "is the worst thing a man could do?"

"Murder, I suppose."

"Aw, I dunno," said Slim. "I've seen murder. It ain't so bad. It's over quick, anyways. But what about a gent that loves a girl and marries the wrong woman. Ain't that about as bad as you can think?"

I did not know, at that time, what Slim had overheard. I was inclined to smile, but this touch of idealism in the boy sobered me.

"It *is* a very great crime," said I, and the thought of Lew Melody and Sandy Furnival did not enter my stupid head! That I had confirmed Slim in his secret thoughts never occurred to me; but his determination was simply that he must save his friend from the dark of hell itself by preventing this marriage with the daughter of Cordoba.

TWENTY-SIX

From a secret coign of vantage, Slim watched the return of Lew Melody to the house of Cordoba. And he saw enough in the manner of Lew to convince him that what he had heard at the door of the house of Furnival was not an illusion, but a gloomy fact. For Melody did not sweep down the street at the full and reckless speed of the Gray Pacer, whirling a cloud of dust behind him, but a dreary and a trudging gait, as though the horse beneath him were exhausted with much work. And yet the Pacer was fairly dancing to be off and away at the full of his stride.

Something had happened in the mind of Melody like the drawing of a curtain which darkens a room. From the window of the Cordoba house, a silvery voice called, and Lew Melody looked up with a smile to Juanita. But it was a forced smile, and an observer as keen as the hidden boy could not fail to note the difference.

All that he saw convinced him more and more.

He decided that there was new and perhaps greater trouble coming, which inspired him to do two things. The first was to run to a Mexican restaurant and there eat the quickest and most filling meal he could get—which was a few tortillas wrapped around cold frijoles. That meal would have been lead in the stomach of any other than Slim, but he returned untroubled to his post from which he could survey comfortably the whole front of the Cordoba house, without being seen in return. There he curled up and fell into a semisleep, for this young animal, like any fox, could sleep with his eyes partly open— as one might say. At least, he was perfectly capable of doing all but lose consciousness while he kept his observance upon one point. That point was the house of Cordoba.

He had an animal patience, too. No cat ever starved and waited by the hole of a mouse with more equanimity, apparently, than did young Slim. For one thing, he was very tired, and therefore he remained in that semisleep the more easily. His place was the flat top of a roof, sheltered from view from the street by another projecting and overlapping eaves above him. Here he remained for long hours. Sometimes he roused enough to change sides and curl into a new position of comfort. Otherwise there was no change. But his skinny body was drinking up rest as the desert drinks up rain.

At length he saw the form of the person for whom he was waiting slip out from the patio gate of the Cordoba house. Slim was instantly wide awake. What he had seen was no more than a dull silhouette, for it was now late at night, and there was nothing but the shining of the bright mountain stars and an occasional yellow bar of lamplight that struck softly across the street. He was very cold as he sat up on the housetop and yawned and stretched the sleep from his body.

But, in the meantime, he was using his eyes industriously. There was no room for doubt. Even if the outline of the man had not been familiar to him, he would have known the furtive lightness of step with which the other now turned down the street—he would have known the very speed of that walk.

Instantly Slim was out of this spy's nest. He dropped down the face of that house like a wild mountain goat jumping from ledge to ledge. So Slim lowered himself to the ground in an unbroken streak. And he set off in pursuit of his friend, Lew Melody, for it was he.

Never was there such anxious caution as that of Slim at this moment, for he knew by the very manner of Melody that, no matter what his goal, it was one to which he wished to go unaccompanied. And when one is shadowing a fox, there is need of more than foxlike cunning. If Lew Melody was a drifting shadow that went rapidly down the street, Slim was a shadow also. His bare feet gave him a great advantage. There was no possibility of striking out a noise as his heel dislodged a small stone. It was as though he were equipped with another pair of eyes in his toes, that told him beforehand the nature of the ground over which he was passing.

They were out of the skirts of the town before Slim had the least idea to what the trail might lead him. For when they were clear of the house, Lew Melody went straight for the heavily-wooded river bottom.

Slim crouched behind the corner of a fence, took counsel with himself, and he was quaking in every fiber of his being. He understood, now. For he was not ignorant of the stories which had been alive in Barney Valley during the last eight years, of how Lew Melody rescued himself from ennui by hunting trouble in the "jungles" of the Barney River bottom lands. In those tangles of willow, the floating life of crime that moved up and down the valley on the trail to Mexico and out again, paused to recruit itself. From those darkly forested places, there issued the covert figures which stole into the town to pilfer what they could lay their hands on.

It was on that account that every yard in Barneytown contained a dog as fierce and as formidable as the pocketbook of the house owner could afford to buy. It was on that account that the streets of the town were deserted at night. Nothing but petty crimes were to be feared, to be sure, for the criminals, with greater thoughts in their hearts, postponed the execution of them until they came to more favorable sections of the country. It was the fear of this same night prowler who advanced in front of Slim, that restrained them. Time was when they had come up out of the tramp jungles of the bottom lands and committed wild and nameless crimes in the little village. But that time was gone. The fear of the law had been impressed upon them by a man more wild and more tigerish than they themselves—Lew Melody!

I, of course, have never seen him in his element. And how much would I not have given to have seen him that night, as Slim saw him, gliding on without sound, scanning all things around him with piercing glances, and never knowing what dark alley mouth, or what fence corner, or what copse of trees, or what thicket of brush, contained enemies on the lookout for him and ready to shoot.

It was very long after this that Slim told me all the thoughts that passed through his mind as he lay there at the corner of the fence, watching his hero pass on down toward the darkness of the bottom lands; and I, hearing them, could understand and sympathize. It was like stepping of one's own free will into the region of a nightmare! And, for a time, Slim hesitated, while the form in front of him first faded and then was lost in the dark of the first trees.

But the instant his eyes lost sight of the man, Slim knew that he could not let him go on alone. He started out at once and ran fast through the dark—fast but softly, as only Slim knew how to run. He wound through the blackness of the copse into which Lew Melody had run—until something sprang on him from behind like a beast of prey, and struck him to the earth.

There had never been a time when Slim had been handled like this. Not even the brutal force of Stan Geary, when that monster used him like a slave, had so paralyzed Slim. He was caught in hands that bit through flesh to the bone with the strength of their hold. And, in an instant, Slim was helpless, pinned down upon his face.

He had only one thought—of Miguel Azatlan.

And then he heard the voice of Lew Melody, turned to iron: "Slim!"

He was too shocked to make any reply, and so he found himself picked up by the back of the neck and dragged into the dim starlight of a clearing. He was set upon his feet and stood, wavering, before this changed man.

Be sure that this was not that Lew Melody who had been saved from a great peril, on a day, by the testimony of Slim in a courtroom. It was not that man, but quite another—an animal of glistening eyes and stern face, a pantherlike creature with no human tenderness in his soul.

"You've followed me, Slim," said Melody.

"I follered you," admitted Slim, shaking.

"D'you know what I came within an ace of doing?" asked Melody, towering above the youngster. "I came within an ace of putting a bullet in you and letting you die."

"Lew," said the boy, "I didn't mean no harm."

"But I did," answered Melody. "I had the knife ready when I jumped at you, Slim. And only by the grace of God I knew when my hand gripped you that you were a boy and not a man. Otherwise you'd be lying back yonder with your throat cut and a few heaps of dead leaves kicked over you. What do you mean by trailing me?"

"I meant nothing wrong," muttered poor Slim.

"You meant nothing wrong?" snarled out Lew Melody. "You meant nothing wrong! Why, you young fool, I knew that I was being shadowed the moment that I left the town, and before that. I knew that I was being followed from the gate of Cordoba's house, and I waited until I could hunt the hunter."

A chill struck through the body of Slim.

"How could you tell, Lew?" he faltered. For he was certain that he had not been seen.

"How can you tell when there's a cold wind blowing on your back?" asked Lew Melody.

"I didn't know," said Slim. "But I thought that you was heading for trouble. That's why I—"

"Why did you think that? Why did you watch the Cordoba house?"

"Who said that I watched it?"

"For hours—or you wouldn't have seen me leave it."

"I only happened along—"

"You lie. And what made you think that I was started for trouble? Slim, I think that you've done a worse thing than lie to me today! And if you have—" He paused, breathing hard. "Go back from the river bottom," said Lew Melody. "Don't try to trail me again. Because if you do, I'll make you wish that you were never born. Now, run for it!"

And Slim turned and ran—ran as if a ghost were pursuing him.

TWENTY-SEVEN

Look in with me upon a little domestic scene in the river bottom near our town, on this night when Lew Melody went on his last man hunt.

It was a clearing on the bank of the river, which runs broad and smooth around a bend, at this point, with its quiet shallows at the edges, dotted with stars. There had been a big and cheerful fire earlier in the night—a fire which tossed armfuls of leaping flames far higher than the tops of the big trees around the clearing. That flaring light made every tree stand out as cold and bright as the sun on a stormy day when the clouds are herded fitfully across its face. But now the great fire had fallen away to an extensive bed of coals which cast a soft light through the clearing, and the trees were solid with shadow. Still, in the center of the open space, near the fire, there was warmth enough, and there was light enough for men to sit in comfort and talk, smoke, and play cards. And that is what they were doing, the six men of this party.

First there was a long, lean man with a grave and thoughtful face, smoking a cigarette with half-shut eyes, as though he were seeing, in his dreams, another scene than this; and beside him a bull-necked fellow had spread out a little sewing kit and was busily mending a rent in his coat, which he had taken off and held in his lap. From time to time, he lifted the coat and examined his work with a careful scrutiny, to see whether he was mending smoothly enough. Just beyond them was a jovial face—a very youthful face with gray hair in odd contrast above it. He had his arms locked around his knees, and he was talking softly—telling his yarn in such a quiet voice that he would not disturb the game of blackjack which continued near by.

At this game, which was played upon a spread-out slicker, sat the two brothers— Miguel and Cristobal Azatlan. But with them was an American who wore a derby hat, oddly out of keeping in such surroundings as these. He was a pale, sickly-looking youth, with the long fingers of an artist.

It was a very quiet scene, and there was no noise except the voice of the narrator, just raised above the silky flow of Barney River.

Let me introduce you to these men again, by name and nature. The grave gentleman with the lean face was Doc Ransom, a confidence man of the old school, and what he dreamed of was the palmy height of his career, when he sat in far other company than this, and spent the money which he had cheated out of the pockets of better men than himself. The bull-necked individual was Tony Mack, who not only understood how to use a needle as well as any housewife, but who was also expert in certain devices which would lift the door from a safe. He had performed these operations in many of the largest cities in the country, and he was now destined, after a streak of bad luck, for the flourishing city of El Paso, where luck and dollars would flow back upon him again. The third of this trio in the foreground was also a known man, for he of the rubicund face and the gray hair was none other than "Smiling" Dan Harper, whose greatest accomplishment was his ability to get his gun out of the holster before the other man, and then shoot quicker and straighter. He had demonstrated his ability in so many lands that sundry sheriffs all over the West were very tired of his exploits in self-defense. He dared not kill again without risking his neck at the end of a hangman's rope. But still, behind those pleasant, smiling eyes, there was the consuming passion—the same passion, in a way, that was now leading Lew Melody toward this very spot!

The Azatlan brothers are already known to you, and he who was playing with them, the sickly youth with the hands of an artist, was a boy from great New York, two thousand miles away. He was a talented youngster who began in a small way as a sneak thief, but, while he was still in his teens, he formed the more exciting habit of walking into small stores in outlying districts of the great town and presenting his gun under the nose of the fear-stricken clerk while he demanded the proceeds of the cash drawer. But, having served a sentence—abbreviated for good behavior—he reverted to his earlier talents in a modified form and became a second-story man, able to open a window without sound, and able to smell out the hidden treasures of a home in their most secret places. He, also, had had a streak of bad luck, but he was turning his face toward more southern and more profitable scenes.

This was the sextet who waited in the hollow clearing for the coming of Lew Melody—though, if they knew that he was at hand—if they knew that he was at this moment lurking at the edge of the forest, watching and weighing them one by one with an unerring instinct—you may be sure that they would not sit so quietly, but would scatter to the trees like so many frightened rabbits.

"Psst!" came the warning hiss of one of the gamblers.

And, at the same moment, a light-stepping shadowy form of a man came out from the trees and approached the glow of the fire.

Miguel Azatlan, having seen him most recently, knew him first and gave his brother the tidings in a murmur which was nevertheless heard plainly by all the rest:

"Be ready, Cristobal! That is Señor Melody!"

Tod Gresham, the boyish second-story man and nimble-fingered thief, was so filled with alarm that he jumped half to his feet and prepared to bolt for the woods. It was the long arm of Doc Ransom, the confidence man, that darted out and caught him and dragged him back to the ground.

"It's Melody!" gasped out the robber.

"Maybe it is. But here are six of us," said Doc Ransom. "Sit tight, my boy. We may need one another, but we don't need to run. Sit still, and watch, and shake your gun loose, so you can get it quick!"

This admirable advice was received by the youthful thief with a shudder of distaste. It was true that he went armed and that he had worked with the trigger of a gun as much as most men of his profession. And yet he had no liking for this work which seemed about to lie ahead of them.

"Guys like you," he snarled softly to Doc, "are just the sort that he uses for his meat—leave your hands off that kale!"

The last was directed to Cristobal Azatlan who, seeing that there was a momentary disturbance, decided to profit by raking in all the stakes which were on the slicker and pocketing them. At the bark of Tod Gresham, he refrained, with a rolling up of his eyes like the glare of a bull before it charges.

In the meantime, Lew Melody had advanced into the rich circle of the firelight and hailed them with a sort of quiet cordiality: "Hello, boys!"

"How's things?" said Ransom.

And: "Señor," murmured the two Mexicans.

They were sitting close together, these two dark-eyed sons of trouble, and lean Miguel whispered at the ear of his half brother: "Why not now, brother?"

"Is your gun ready?"

"I shall use a knife. I trust it more."

"No! While you draw back your arm to throw the knife—even if you are quicker than a striking snake, he will have his

251

revolver out and he will kill us both! We must work with guns only."

"As you please. But quickly. I am nervous, brother."

"Not yet! See how cool the devil is! Perhaps he has friends yonder in the brush. If he did not have them there, how would he dare to come in this way to six of us?"

"True!"

"One of us must try to come behind him—or else, one on either side of him. Then watch me—when I start my hand, start yours. One of us he is sure to kill. I hope it is I, not you, my brother."

"As God wills, so must it be. Farewell!"

"Farewell, brother. We shall never speak to one another again in this world!"

So, in whispers inaudible a foot away, quickly, with the resignation of stoics, they determined to kill or be killed.

Lew Melody, in the meantime, had entered into a cheering conversation with the others.

Smiling Dan Harper led the talk with: "We hear that you aim to settle down, Melody?"

"Is that what marriage means?" said Melody.

"I suppose so."

"Well, you ought to know, Harper!"

"You know me?" cried Dan Harper in surprise, and in alarm also.

"Oh, yes."

"How does that happen?"

"I knew Sam Arnold."

"Was he a friend of yours?" asked Harper, his voice becoming a little strained.

"We used to have fist fights when I was a kid. Well, I don't think that I could call him a friend. Did he put up a real fight with you?"

Don Harper hesitated an instant. It was two years ago that he had killed Sam Arnold. The face and the voice of that unlucky boy floated back upon his memory too vividly.

"It was a bad evening's work for me," said Harper, watching the face of his inquisitor with a sort of critical anxiety. "We'd been drinking, and then we started playing cards. I thought that Sam had too much luck. And he said that it was just the swing of the cards. But when a feller wins seven hands running—well, you know, Melody."

"Sure," said Melody, with the utmost

good nature. "Some one said that you shot him under the table."

The face of Dan Harper contracted. "As I was jumpin' the gun out of the leather, the darn thing went off—"

"I understand," said Lew Melody, and smiled. "They tell me that you got two more slugs into Arnold as he was droppin' to the floor."

"That's a lie, and a loud lie! I'd like to get the dirty dog that told it!"

"Maybe it is. It's a queer thing how facts are lost when a story has been told a few times, isn't it, Dan?"

"You're right," declared Dan, welcoming this friendly tone.

And he felt that there might well be a reason behind this friendliness. If Melody had come into the jungle bent on action, he certainly could not wish to attack all six of them at the same time. He must establish a friendship with a few of them—or a state of neutrality, at least.

"To say that I'd shoot a man that was down!" cried Harper. "That's a rotten thing to spread around. I'd like to get the rat who said it."

"I've forgotten," said Lew. "It was some

fellow from Montana. He told us quite a lot about you."

"What else?"

"Why, I remember that he said that Shep McArthur was a friend of yours."

Here Tony Mack, whose glittering eyes had never left the face of the young gun fighter, broke in: "Well, that was the truth. You and Shep was bunkies, Dan. Ain't that right?"

"We was," admitted Harper. "He was my best friend in the world. He left me one summer. Heaven knows whatever became of him!"

"I can tell you," said Lew Melody, "one part of the story. I met him right here. There was a fire that night a good deal like this one tonight. I remember that Shep McArthur was boss of the fire and was telling the boys what to do. He told me to get some wood for the fire, and he spoke very sharply. I'm a very sensitive, nervous sort of a chap, Harper. When he spoke to me that way, I couldn't help objecting. And in another moment—you know how it is—we had our guns out. I was unlucky enough to hit him with the first shot."

He was speaking with an oiled gentleness, but the eyes which he fastened upon

Dan Harper were the eyes of a tiger. He held the entire group fascinated.

"That bullet went through his leg, Dan. He shouted that he had enough as he dropped, and I stopped shooting, of course. But the minute he saw me lower my gat, he raised his and starting pumping lead at me as he lay on the ground. His bullet nicked my ear. I'll always remember McArthur because of the chip on the rim of this ear." He touched the place gently with his fingers.

"So you understand, Dan, why I had to kill him?"

"I understand," said Dan Harper huskily. And all the muscles in his throat were distended by the grip of his teeth as he ground them together.

"I'll sit down by you, Mack," said Melody, "if you don't mind." And he made himself comfortable by the fire—sitting at the extreme point of the arc of which Cristobal Azatlan made the other tip.

"You know me, too?" said Mack.

"I know that Dan Harper and Tony Mack often travel together," said Lew. "That's why I suppose that you're Tony Mack."

"Our friend seems to be a mind reader!"

exclaimed Doc Ransom, who had been using the last conversational interval to shift his gun to a more convenient pocket. "He seems to be able to select names for all of us! What about our two friends on the left? Could you name them?" said Doc Ransom.

"Miguel and Cristobal Azatlan," said Lew Melody. "We have met before. I might almost say that we are old friends. I knew their brother a year ago!"

The deadly irony of this remark caused even the calm of Doc Ransom to break a little, and he flashed a side glance at the two Mexicans. But they sat with faces of stone, smoking and hearing nothing.

"And here is another," said Ransom, pointing to Tod, the sneak thief and burglar. "You have given four names out of six, and I suppose that you could name this gentleman, also?"

Perhaps I have pointed out that Lew Melody had, one by one, created enemies out of four of the six men in the circle around the fire. It was impossible, surely, that he could intend to throw down the glove to the entire six! But now he lighted a cigarette, and waved an open path through the mist of his first expelled breath so that he might study Tod Gresham more intently.

"I don't know your name, partner," said the gentle voice of Lew Melody, "but I can tell how you make your living."

Tod started nervously. "Tell me, then!" said he, filled with defiance.

"Why, that's easy enough. You make your living with your hands—and yet you don't work."

The sneak thief clenched his fists and glared at the other, but after a moment's reflection, he decided that if such a formidable warrior as Dan Harper had decided to pocket up a cause for battle, certainly he, Tod Gresham, could afford to follow that example.

"You have named four and the occupation of a fifth," said Doc Ransom, turning his cool glance straight upon Melody. "And what about me?"

"You're another who hates work," said Lew Melody. "Talk is enough for you, is it not? You can talk money out of the purses of other men, I suppose!"

It was the final blow. One by one, he had slapped each of the six in the face!

TWENTY-EIGHT

When Slim bolted away from Lew Melody, he had no thoughts of turning back, after a little time, and attempting to resume the trail. For he felt very much as though he had walked after a tamed house cat and found it transformed suddenly into a panther. The thought of that stalking panther drove him on until his breath failed and then he slowed to a walk. His feet were now in the velvet dust of the old town, and that softness was grateful to them, for as the ecstasy of fear subsided in him, he was aware that they were cut and bleeding and tingling with pain—with such abandon had he raced through the dark of the night.

He paused, finally, to take stock of possibilities. What he was convinced of was that Lew Melody had gone out to throw away his life because life had become a burden to him; and, in some way, this thing must be avoided. All that he could think of on the spur of the moment was to go to the house of Cordoba—not that Cordoba himself was a fighting man who could rescue Slim's hero, but Cordoba was rich, and Slim knew that money works with a thousand strong hands.

, So he went to the black-faced house of the moneylender, where the stars struck out a few high lights out of the blank windows. He knocked at the front door, first, but he got no response. Then he clambered to the balcony and tapped again, loudly, at the upper door which opened upon that balcony.

Finally he heard muffled voices. Then a light gleamed inside the room and the voice of Cordoba, shaken with excitement, called: "Who's there?"

"Slim!" said the boy.

A lamp was suddenly interposed between the curtain and the window of the door, so that a strong shaft of light struck out upon Slim, leaving the holder of the lamp in darkness. Then the door was unfastened and opened.

"What do you wish, young man?" said Cordoba, repressing stronger language because he knew that Slim was a close friend to Lew Melody.

"I want help for Lew," said the boy. "He—"

"What sort of help for a man soundly

asleep—too soundly asleep to hear your rapping?" growled out Cordoba, yawning.

"Go look in his room, if you don't believe me," said Slim, furious at every delay.

Cordoba scanned him once again—cast an anxious glance around the room to make sure that there was nothing this young vagabond could steal when his back was turned, and then hurried to the room of Melody. He opened the door and then came hurrying back, this time with a pale face.

"He is not here!" muttered Cordoba. "He is not here. But I saw him go his room—how—"

"He's in the river bottom!"

"No, no!" groaned Cordoba. "He vowed that he would give up such—how can you know that he is there?"

"I follered him till he found me out and sent me back. He's bound for the river bottom, and to raise the devil there!"

"Ah," groaned the unhappy man, "why should he do such a thing as that—now!"

"Because he ain't happy," said Slim, trembling with emotion.

"We saw that he was moody tonight—all young men will be that way. They are like calves or colts! They have whims. But—boy, do you know that his marriage is less than a week away?"

"And ain't that the thing that's eatin' him now?" cried Slim.

"Diablo!" gasped out Cordoba, and could say no more, while he stared at Slim as at a ghost.

"Where was he today?" went on Slim bitterly. "Where did he go today?"

"To Señor Furnival, yes. But what of that?"

"To Furnival? The devil, no! Maybe he seen Furnival—but the one he stayed to talk to was Sandy!"

Cordoba put down the lamp because his hand had begun to shake so that he dared not continue holding it.

"You are talking of something that means more than your words," said the moneylender. "Ah, may we keep sorrow from Juanita's life! A blow is about to fall; I have felt it, and I have dreaded its coming! Boy, tell me whatever you know!"

"I know that Lew Melody is eatin' his heart out because he's got to marry Juanita," said Slim.

There is little tact in boys. Besides, Slim was desperate. It was the picture of Lew

Melody's peril that crushed him, not the troubles of the old moneylender. And when Cordoba stretched out his hands in appeal and cried: "How can that be?" the answer of Slim was brutally to the point.

"Because it's Sandy that he loves—don't everybody love her? And ain't Lew the only gent that she ever looked at?"

In this great crisis, Cordoba gathered all his strength and became calm. "Speak softly," said he. "If there is any truth in what you say—but there cannot be! But not a whisper of it must be heard in this house—or it would turn my home into a hell! Now tell me how you could know this? But you could not know! It is a guess—a dream!"

"Cordoba," said Slim fiercely, "I heard 'em talkin'. I stood at the door when they thought I was a mile away, and I heard 'em talkin'."

Cordoba sank into a chair and supported his face in both uncertain hands.

"It is the end!" groaned he. "It is the black day of our three lives! What is my sin that this should be done to me now? But he—treacherous devil! He has crept like a snake into the heart of my girl!"

"He done the right thing as he seen it,"

said Slim. "When Juanita rode up to him in the mountains—he had to try to keep her from bein' talked about. He wants to go through with it, but I tell you that after he seen Sandy today, he'd rather die than marry anybody else. I tell you that I stood there and heard 'em talk like they was both gunna die the next minute. And now Lew is down in the river bottom huntin' for trouble—and God knows that he'll find it! Them Azatlans are there, and I know that Tony Mack and Smilin' Dan blew into Barneytown today. He'll run amuck with the whole gang of 'em—unless you do something to stop him!"

"He must be stopped," gasped out Cordoba, staring wildly about him. "Think for me, my boy! Find a way! How shall I do it?"

"Ain't you got a house full of servants? Ain't you got friends? Get half a dozen gents with guns and send 'em for the bottom lands. They'll find him there, and I'll be one of the gang. I'll do as big a share as any other man—only, by myself, I couldn't handle Lew tonight. He's gone sort of crazy. I thought he was gunna kill me for follerin' him."

The door into the room of Juanita had

opened some moments before, and now she ran out at them, a slender white form.

"It is too late already!" cried she. "Do you hear?"

Up from the river bottom, in the breath of silence that followed, they heard the sudden chattering of guns—many guns in rapid action like a mutter of musketry in the distance. But Cordoba forgot everything else. He ran to his daughter and caught her by the shoulders and turned her so that the light struck across her face.

"What have you heard, Juanita?" groaned he.

"I have heard everything," said she.

"It is all a lie!" moaned Cordoba. "There is no truth in it. You shall not believe, my sweet girl!"

She tore herself away from him. "Why do you speak of me, always!" cried she. "Don Luis is being murdered in the river bottom! Raise the town. Do not wait to saddle the horses. Ride bareback. Ride, ride! I shall come as I can—will you go? Will you stand still and drive me mad!"

And she rushed back into her room.

Her mother came hurrying in as Juanita tore off her nightclothes and began to dress haphazardly. In the distance there was the voice of Cordoba thundering to his neighbors—the sound of other windows opening, with a slam—other voices shouted in reply.

"What are you doing?" sobbed the señora. "Where are you going, Juanita?"

"I am going where I may help him for the last time," said the girl.

"God pity us!"

"Have you heard, too?"

"Everything! But it must be a lie!"

"A lie? I heard the guns in the hollow. And I know that he is dying now."

"You must not go. Juanita—"

The girl knocked away the hands of her mother with a furious strength. "Do not touch me. I *must* go. If I may hear his last words—perhaps he will see my face—the last face in his life—"

"Juanita, it will kill you—it will break your heart! You will die of it!"

"What is *my* life?"

"He has lied and pretended to you—"

"Ah," cried the girl savagely, "if you say such things of him, I could kill you!"

She had dressed while she talked, flinging her clothes upon her body and now, stamping her slender feet into her boots, her short black hair whirling about her head, she rushed past the señora and across the big room, and past the piano where her mother had played while she taught Lew Melody to dance—and to dance his way into the heart of Sandy Furnival.

She thought of these things as she fled down the back stairs of the house. And when she reached the courtyard, she found a swirl of men and horses there—saddling—arming, shouting.

"Don't wait for saddles!" cried Juanita. "There is no time! There are men dying in the river bottom! God reward you if you hurry!"

But, fast as they fled down the road, she was up with the leaders, before they reached the woods. She was up with them, flashing along on the bare back of the pinto mare, which had been given to her by Melody himself.

A reward because she had taught him to dance!

TWENTY-NINE

When Lew Melody had, in his own fashion, insulted the half dozen grim fighters who sat around him, a little pause followed, and during that pause his hand went slowly to his lips and down again, as he puffed at his cigarette.

And all were fascinated by that hand. It was as slender, almost, as the hand of a woman, but the square-tipped fingers and the round wrist, in which the cords thrust out at every movement, told of the gripping strength which was there.

It was neither grace nor beauty in that hand, however, which so charmed the watchers, but the peculiar steadiness with which it moved and, every moment or so, flicked the ashes from the fuming end of the cigarette. For, very obviously, he now stood in danger of his life from six men, and each one of them was capable of struggling like a tiger. Yet he continued his smoking with the same deliberation— even when Miguel Azatlan, rising to put a fresh clump of brush upon the fire, moved to another part of the circle, a point at which he was just opposite to his brother.

But Lew Melody did not appear to see. Neither did he seem to care when the heat of the glowing embers of the fire ignited the dry brush and sent a hissing column of flame aloft in the air, where it stood like an orange pillar, wagging its head and snapping off wild arms of brightness that vanished instantly in the black of the night.

Yet he was now at a greater disadvantage than ever. Only a gunman of such uncanny expertness as himself could have shot with any certainty in the dull light of a moment before, but in the full flare of the fire, each of the six would have immensely improved chances.

No one spoke. And yet the loudest speeches, the most blasphemous insults could not have filled the air with such a tensity of excitement.

Then, from the town, an excited dog began to bark, the noise coming in sharp little pulses through the air and dropping into the clearing.

"Darn that dog!" said Tony Mack.

"I'd like to kill all dogs in the world!" snarled Smiling Dan Harper. "I've had their teeth in my legs too often!"

"Then start right in close to home," muttered Tod Gresham, who was trembling and gasping in a nervous frenzy of excitement.

"Start where?" asked Tony Mack, who was slow of wit.

"Here!" screamed the boy, and snatched at his gun.

When he leveled it, he found that he was covering not Lew Melody, but the squat form of Tony Mack, for at the voice of the boy, Melody had dropped his cigarette and flung himself at Mack. Even that stoutly muscled body was helpless under his handling. They whirled—and Tony Mack staggered helplessly back toward the fire as Melody leaped for the trees.

The first bullet to follow him was that of Tod Gresham. It clipped his coat at the point of the shoulder. The second was from the gun of Miguel Azatlan; and his brother's bullet whirred past the ear of the retreating fighter. But before there was chance for more action, Tony Mack pitched back into the midst of the fire, beat down the flames, scattered the flaring brush far and wide, and threw the whole group into confusion. Tony Mack himself rolled with a scream from that terrible bed and started, still yelling with agony, toward the broad, black coldness of the water.

Lew Melody had turned from his flight toward the trees and dropped flat on the ground with two guns stretched out before him.

His first shot caught the tall body of Miguel Azatlan squarely in the stomach and, plowing through his flesh, broke the backbone. He died without a groan. His second shot landed below the hips of Tod Gresham and passed through both thighs. He fell with a shriek of pain, for his flesh was frightfully torn. Then Melody was up and flying toward the trees again. For there was no other easy target before him. The remaining three—Smiling Dan Harper and Doc Ransom and burly Cristobal Azatlan—had sought better cover by throwing themselves upon the ground in imitation of his own maneuver.

As he ran, he swerved like a football player running through a broken field, and though the bullets sang wickedly around him, he reached the very border of the trees before he was struck.

He did not know where the shot landed. But from head to feet he went numb, while the heavy blow knocked him forward upon his face.

The wild, three-throated yell of the enemy called back his senses from a fog of pain and shock. He turned on the ground and fired at a leaping form which ran toward him, gigantically big and black against the firelight.

That grotesque figure seemed to be

snuffed into nothingness! In reality, Smiling Dan Harper had gone to the ground with a bullet through his head.

But there were two other points of rapidly jetting fire—the weapons of Azatlan and Doc Ransom. Twice, long ripping thrills of flame passed through the flesh of Lew Melody before the sheer agony of pain enabled him to roll into the covering shadows of the trees. He managed to gain hands and knees and so to drag himself behind a trunk.

There he lay with his back to the firelight in the clearing and his face turned toward the heart of the woods, for he had a feeling that if they came at him it would be from the trees.

Presently he heard a crackling farther into the woods. They were searching for him there, not dreaming that the extent of his wounds had chained him to the place to which he had first forced himself.

Somewhere in his body there was a painful pulse, every throb of which was driving life from his body, and he knew that he was fast bleeding to death. He was not sorry for it. It seemed to Lew Melody, as he lay there in the dark, that it was the only way to extricate himself from the frightful tangle of his life; the knot could only be cut. If he had one desire, it was to see the forms of his two last enemies in the sextet come into view and range of his gun.

But that was too much to pray for. Here, in his last and greatest battle, he felt himself dying, and he could not help a certain boyish thrill in the knowledge that the world would talk of this deed long after it had forgotten the work of better men than himself. He had snuffed out two lives and laid another low and held off three more. It was a comfortable night's work even for Lew Melody!

Another crackling in the brush told him that the pair of hunters had turned back toward the edge of the fire. Hunting as they were hunting, stealthily, with a deadly caution, there was little chance that they would fail to see him before he saw them. He made himself ready to accept a bullet; and, in return, he steadied himself and quickened his nerve to drive an answering bullet back at the jet of fire. A little below the tongue of flame he would direct his own aim, for they would doubtless be stretched along the ground.

So he waited, with the life ebbing from

him at every moment. And a lifetime, I suppose, whirled through his brain with the passage of each second.

Then he heard the noise of Tony Mack— frightfully burned, to judge by his groans —as he dragged himself from the water back toward the dry land—a groan for every breath he drew. Perhaps that rascal had been injured enough to end him with the others. There was a grim satisfaction to Lew Melody in that thought.

There was a new sound, now, a distant muttering like soft thunder which rattles beyond the edge of the horizon. But this grew faster than the noise of any thunderstorm sweeping across the face of the sky. It swelled and whirled closer—the pounding of the hoofs of many horses!

Then, with a great crashing, the cavalcade struck the outskirts of the woods.

"Slim!" said Melody to himself. "But it's too late!"

The meaning of that noise was not lost upon the two hunters in the dark. There began a brisk crackling as they rushed from the brush covert in an opposite direction, and at the same time, the first riders lunged into the dull glow of the firelight which filled the clearing. Lew Melody, turning himself with an infinite labor, saw Juanita—the first rider—on the pinto mare which he had given to her.

"Luis!" she cried.

It was not she whom he wished, but since she had come, he answered faintly: "Here!"

She was at his side in a flash, and men thronging after her—a great dismounting, snorting of horses, creaking of leather, jingling of spurs. He was pleased with these sounds. They came to him as out of a sleepy distance, for a black burden of rest was falling upon his eyes.

The face of Juanita, as she leaned above him, was a dull blur. Only her voice had life and light as she spoke to him. And then came her sharp cry of agony.

"Help! He is dying!"

Professional hands took charge of him. Vaguely he recognized the voice of the Mexican doctor. Lights flared up around him. No, he was being carried into the clearing and now he was put down by the fire, which was freshened until it filled the eyes of Lew Melody with yellow lightnings.

Then, from Juanita: "He will live, doctor?"

"I cannot tell," said the doctor. "If he wants to live—perhaps!"

Lew Melody heard no more. He had fallen into a blissful sleep, so it seemed to him—or was it death toward which he sank? No, for he was called back by burning pains. The doctor, with two assistants, was hastily drawing wide, gripping bandages, about his wounds. That pain gathered like a great crescendo of music, and crashed upon his brain.

And he fell into darkness again.

Juanita was not in the clearing. She had remounted the pinto mare and now she was flying up from the river bottom, and twisting through the thick shadows of the Mexican town, and then the hoofs of her horse struck out an echoing roar from the old bridge that staggered across the Barney River.

Before her glowed the lights of the American section, with its broader streets, and now she was passing through it with the scent of freshly watered lawns coming cool and fragrant upon either side. And now she was beyond those lights of the town and stretching up the weary rise of hills to the east.

The pinto mare, laboring, with all her

might, seemed to be standing still, and the girl flogged her onward remorselessly. So, reeling with weakness, completely run out, the pinto reached the house of Furnival, and the shrilling voice of the girl reached the ears of the sleepers in the house; yes, it passed behind the house and, needlelike, pierced the heavy sleep of the men in the bunkhouse beyond the main building.

A moment later and Furnival was at the front door. He opened it upon a wild-eyed creature, trembling, and crying to him: "I must see the Señorita Furnival—quickly, oh quickly! It is the life of Don Luis!"

And here was Sandy herself flying down the stairs, already half dressed, and drawing on the last of her clothes and doing buttons with flying fingers.

"They have shot Don Luis—in the river bottom! Six men—and they have killed him, but he will want to see you before he closes his eyes. He is dying, señorita!"

Here were two races and two different souls face to face, and Sandy was as white and as cool as the Mexican girl was shaken and wailing!

"Will you help me saddle a horse, father?" said she, and was through the door at once.

Furnival, in his nightclothes, followed. It was he who flung the rope that captured the horse; it was she who dragged out saddle and bridle. Between them the animal was instantly ready. And then she was off—no, with the spurs ready to thrust into the flanks of her mount, she stopped to Juanita, standing at her side.

"I understand," said she. "It is more than I could have done for you! God bless you for it!"

Then she was gone.

How she rode that night! I was an eyewitness, for the news from the river bottom had come back on wings to the town, and half of Barneytown was in the saddle, I think—myself among the rest—when a foaming horse flew down the street and some one cried: "Sandy Furnival!"

Like a bolt from the sky, she was past us. I rode as hard as I could, but the thundering hoofs of her horse were on the bridge long before I was there.

I cannot tell how she found her way so straight to the clearing. Perhaps there were other hurrying horsemen already streaming in the same direction, for the whole valley would burn tomorrow with the tale of how

Lew Melody had fought six men hand to hand.

But when she stormed into the hollow, she was met by a deadly silence.

"It is death! I am too late!" said Sandy to her own sick heart.

So she slipped from the saddle and ran to the quiet form beside the towering fire, all of whose ruddiness could not relieve the pallor of his face.

His eyes were closed.

"It is death?" whispered Sandy.

"I cannot tell," said the doctor. "I cannot get the pulse—but there still seems to be a little trace of breath—"

He held the mirror again at the nostrils of Melody.

"Lewis!" said the girl.

And all those who leaned to watch, swore to me afterward that he came far enough back from death in answer to her voice to open his eyes and smile at her.

"The Black Signal," they heard him mutter. "She has come back and I must—" and his voice trailed away into the silence.

Of course Lew Melody lived. If he had not, I should never have been able to draw from him more than half of the odd little details with which I have been able to adorn his history. Of course Lew Melody lived, and Sandy married him.

She is coming in this afternoon, for since the death of Mrs. Cheswick, she has led the singing.

But now, as I come toward the end, I wonder what is balanced in this narrative—sorrow or happiness? And has the happiness of the Melodys been great enough to counterbalance the anguish which uprooted the Cordobas from their home and sent their three lives south to Mexico?

Sandy still writes to Juanita and hears from her from time to time. Mrs. Cordoba did not live long in Mexico City. And Cordoba himself has failed rapidly. As for the girl herself, twice it seems that she had been prepared for a marriage, and twice something has happened to break off the match. And, though Juanita does not confess what it is, I suppose that by this time we all know.

We look at Lew Melody, grown more brown and prosperous than any of us dreamed possible, and we understand.

The publishers hope that this
Large Print Book has brought
you pleasurable reading.
Each title is designed to make
the text as easy to see as possible.
G.K. Hall Large Print Books
are available from your library and
your local bookstore. Or, you can
receive information by mail on
upcoming and current Large Print Books
and order directly from the publishers.
Just send your name and address to:

G.K. Hall & Co.
70 Lincoln Street
Boston, Mass. 02111

or call, toll-free:

1-800-343-2806

A note on the text
Large print edition designed by
Kristina Hals
Composed in 16 pt Plantin
on a Xyvision 300/Linotron 202N
by Genevieve Connell
of G.K. Hall & Co.

ACP
2-W
2 7. 16